I0600148

A Familiar Future

By Parker Hilton

For all the greats who came before me and those who will

come after me.

And for my grandmother, who passed away too young

Prologue

This May 8th, 2086, the date of my birth. For whomever it may concern,

I write in this diary deep in the Amazon rainforest. I did not originally want this book; I received it as a present and saw it silly and pointless. Surprisingly though, something occurred to me soon after gaining it. I do not know who will read this, or if it is even necessary. But I feel that my story needs to be written, it seemed unjust for it not to be told. I am a scientist you see, and I wish to record my findings. My name is Juan Cortezeon, and today I am 68 years old. Though it may seem close to the end of my life, I plan on making many more discoveries. I am an infamous scientist, known around the world, and these past months my goal has been to save my homeland of the Andy Region (recently formed after the collapse of the U.S.) and search for new plant and wildlife.

Myself, along with a team of fellow explorers, have made much progress down the Amazon River but have stopped due to rainfall. The rain is loud against the soft tarp above my head. Leaking onto this very book. However, I must go now; the rain is slowing down. For whomever may find this book I know they will cherish it, for I am Juan Cortezeon. A gift to humanity.

May 26th, 2086,

I have been in this wretched jungle for too long! We have been walking for days in the thick brush; five men have already died. Disease, creatures, and even plants have ravaged us. Of course, all my men are expendable. I have gotten what I have come for, new species unknown to man before me! You see, as I said, I am a gift to humanity. 15 species! Eight plants and seven animals! Of course, the animals are small creatures, nothing more than insects. The plants are what I am most interested in, from a scientific standpoint a new plant is just a dollar sign. Who knows, some new drug could come from any of the following organisms. We will have to see.

June 5th, 2086,

I am back in North America now, in my own lab named in my honor, the Juan Cortezeon Institute, in San Francisco. I have been doing many studies on the plants I have collected and have named a few. None have any useful properties it seems, except one. I have dubbed it the

Cortezeon Plant. It will take further studying to determine exactly what it does, but I have a guess. If my hypothesis is right, this plant and I, could change the world.

October18th, 2086,

I have failed. I have lost my grant, and my institute. My expedition was a bust. The plant that I was wishing to study, when added to mammal life forms, has no obvious effect. I gave ten rats the plant, each one of them is living completely normally. I debated throwing this diary away, for it reminds me of my failures, but I kept it. I felt that my thoughts needed to be written down, my legacy needed to endure… Goodbye for now.

January 7th, 2094,

Oh, what a joyous occasion, I am seventy-five now, but I feel as young as ever. My name as a scientist has been redeemed. Those rats, which I so long ago gave the Cortezeon Plant to have just recently died. Four times the average life span! It is a miracle that I kept this journal (along with the rats). I do not know what this drug will do to the human body, I have just started studying, but I plan on finding out. I am once again reminded of my importance.

January 12th, 2094,

I have already completed half my studies, and it seems I have found a drug which cheats death! I am so happy; the world will know my name once again and...

February 2nd, 2094,

I am no longer in my lab. Currently, I am in a hospital chair. My wife is in a bed beside me, a cancer plagues her. You would think I would be upset but I am not. I don't know why, and that seems to upset me the most. That I cannot figure out my own miraculous brain.

Some say I feel this way because I think too highly of myself, but I simply blame my mind. It's high superiority

*to others just means I have evolved past human emotions.
Besides, my wife will be fine, I have already given her a
dose of my drug. If my studies are as they seem, she will be
well in a few days.*

February 20th, 2094,

*My wife is dead on this day. Again though, I feel no
loss. Maybe everyone is right, maybe I have become too
self-centered, believing I am the most important person
alive, but I refuse to think this. So, the medication doesn't
cure people, it doesn't matter. I think the plant can and will
be used for something.*

February 27, 2094,

*I was at my wife's funeral today, and something
touched me. Her death has just now hit me, and my tears
splash down on this page. Now I need this drug to work, I
need people to stop feeling the pain I am feeling now. I will
update you when this has finally been achieved.*

March 8th, 2144,

My drug, the Cortezeon Plant, has already worked miracles as I predicted. It does not cure people as I previously suspected, it expands life! People have already begun taking my drug as a one dose pill given to those eighteen years and up. I am now 126 years old; the population has become 10 billion. With a growing population, space was needed, so of course forests were cut down, but it is all necessary for the advancements of humanity. And this drug will only cause mankind to excel. The average lifespan is now 240 years, it doesn't heal as I originally thought, but human beings have almost reached immortality.

November 1st, 2253,

Population 20 billion. I may have been wrong. Every time I pick up this diary it seems the world changes drastically, yet humankind remains in a similar state to what it has always been. Very few parks are left,

advancements have slowed, war is everywhere, trees

become scarcer, and almost every building has become an

apartment. I miss my wife now, more than ever.

July 26th, 2300,

It is our country's birthday today, and yet I don't

feel patriotic. It seems the Andy Region has forgotten its

people. I feel alone, even though the population has

become 25 billion. The last time I saw a plant well... I

cannot say. All things beautiful are gone. I could go to the

zoo, animals and plants are tightly housed there (though

the price is too high). A new law had been implemented due

to a small scare. All genetic testing and forms of

bioengineering are illegal, both of which I love. Some of my

work too, which relates to genetic research has been

purged along with others like it. I should have been killed

just for being an expert of the science, but I have become a sort of idol now. The whole world knows my name, they thank me, worship me. I wish they did not.

June 5th, 2386,

It has been three hundred years since I came into possession of this book. Sadly, this diary, though it's age, is not much different than technology today. Tech. has barely advanced since the end of the 21st century; we have become too focused on wars to even develop anything. All the same machines and computers as when I was a boy.

I am on my death bed now, and I regret everything. I miss my wife, I have poisoned the Earth and cursed us all. And yet no one seems to notice. The country doesn't either. I once said I was infamous... I am not. Here at the end, I realize how small we all are. We are miniscule, and anyone who thinks we are important, or worthy, is wrong. We may be the dominant species, we may have a population over 30 billion, but we are small. No one else seems to realize. And so, I write this so that someone in the future will stop this corrupt world.

This document will be destroyed; I am sure of it. Not just because there is no one who knows me personally anymore, but also because of this corrupt government. When seeing my treason (though such a small act, saying the country doesn't care about us) they will hate me for it. And so, for whomever it may concern, farewell. Though I know that in the future someone who believes in this cause will make a difference. Someone the complete opposite of me, someone who realizes, before it is too late, how small we are. Because until humanity can realize how small we are compared to the rest of the universe we are a lost species.

100 years later

Chapter 1

Grass. So much grass. Sky, so much sky. The air felt crisp and cool, fresher than any mint. What a world. I could hear the birds tweeting, the wind rustling the leaves in the trees--

"*Er. Er. Er!*"

I put my hand on my cold metal alarm clock, and I rocketed back to the real world. I looked outside hoping to see what I had seen in my dream, but all I saw was what I always saw: grey clouds, grey concrete, and grey water. The average color of the Andy Region, and at that, the world.

I frowned; this was a dream I had had often. A dream that I wished could be my reality. But just a dream, I reminded myself. Nothing more. Sometimes it was best not to hope too much in such a world as I lived in. So, I lay there, unmoving, staring up at the fan of my dorm as it went around and around. Almost hypnotizing me, recreating the world I had just left. Transporting me to another, more peaceful place. I sighed as I blinked, rubbing the sleep from my eyes.

During mornings like these, when I woke up just before the busy day, I liked to think about my dreams while lying in bed. About that strange and yet familiar place. A place which might have once been, a place I wished to go.

A thought hit me as I was doing this, and I clambered out of bed. I was free today; I could visit Tim! I quickly got dressed in my military uniform, the smallest size, freshened my breath, put my green military hat on my blond hair, and ran out of the door. I stopped to look in the mirror for a second, my young face shining back, though of course, like the rest of the population I was ancient.

Opening the door, I stepped out into a white room with lights that would occasionally flicker out only to come back on. Towards the back of the room was the front desk, where under a big sign labeled, *Check Out*, sat an old woman with glasses, a pen in one hand, and a cigarette in the other. I had to peer over the desk. "Good morning, Janet!" I said excitedly.

"Brian Watson," replied the old woman, not looking up from her work. "I know you want to see your son, but it is five in the morning. He is not going anywhere. Will you at least let me wake up with a cigarette!"

"Please just check me out."

"Fine," said Janet, puffing smoke into my pale face covered in freckles as she wrote on a piece of paper. I wrinkled my nose.

I walked out of the institute smiling and skipping. I looked back at the sign which was above the doors I had walked out of. It read: *Juan Cortezeon Military Institute*. It felt good to finally get out of that horrible building.

As I walked farther and farther away from the institute, looking back at the concrete building, I remembered that the outside didn't look much different. Everything was the same shade as the concrete, the tall skyscrapers, the grey sky which let in minimal sunlight, and the grey water which splashed up onto the docks. The sight was enough to make a day that should be wondrous, awful. The only color difference was the people. So many people. I had trouble weaving in and around the crowds of people. Skin touching skin. I was being pushed around; I tried to make my way to the sidewalk (those were occasionally less crowded), but I kept getting pushed in the wrong direction. And everyone knew what would happen if you stopped. You would be trampled, nobody would help you, no one cared. In this world you were always lonely, yet never alone…

My only anchor was the speck of green on the horizon, just above the city and the shore. A handful of evergreens and tall grasses. I had never stopped wondering what it was. A small park perhaps? Maybe even a forest high up in the hills? It didn't matter; I just liked to look at it because it gave me a calming feeling when walking through the chaos. Sometimes, I even liked to imagine there was a cabin up in those trees, and that one day I might live out my days in peace.

Once, I had tried to go up there and see for myself what that land harbored, see if my wildest hopes and dreams could become reality. However, a chain link fence surrounded the small patch, and I was only able to get close enough to smell the air of pine. Nothing but a small whiff, unable to even glance at what type of wonders were being hidden from me. Hid for (most likely) some kind of government testing which the public was not allowed to know about. I even contemplated breaking in, but could not bring myself to violate the A.R.'s laws.

What surprised me was that even though the Andy Region controlled both Americas, and some of Antarctica, we were still very compact. The A.R. was formed when the U.S., and other nations, were destroyed in the third world war, in the year 2054. It was said that the United States had been corrupt and needed to be stopped. So, the A.R. had taken control. Their policies were the same, and in truth I sometimes thought they were just as corrupt as the nations before us.

Everyone knew that way back, things were different. Less people, more trees and animals. People cared about others, there was religion. The sky was once blue, or at least that was the rumor. The ocean was plentiful. And humans lived alongside nature. I always thought that all would be weird though. Yet deep down, somewhere in our genes, I believe all humans have the same feeling, the same idea: I know the world I see before me is not right.

I continued down the street, dodging the homeless in their ragged clothes who sat on the pavement. One person, a mother with three children, dressed in a torn shirt, looked up at me in dismay. I smiled. "Here you go," I said, dropping coins into the mother's hands.

"Thank you, sir!" The mother sobbed out.

Tipping my green cap in her direction, I kept on walking. Though I strongly disliked the military, they housed me, fed me, and paid me. Without them I would be living on the streets like the people before me.

I turned my head to look up at the dreary sky which was dotted with buildings and air taxis. Across billboards and skyscrapers, the Andy Range flag waved, a green Earth with two parallel lines intersecting it along with President Kyle's handsome face in the corner of it. I put my hand in the air, signaling to one of the vehicles. I watched as it flew down, stopping to hover mere feet from the ground.

I walked up to the white machine. It had two propellers on either side that could rotate to hover in the air or go forward, and a tail propellor to change direction. On my side of the taxi was the company's name: *T-Flyer*. I put a couple of the standard, pink, A.R. dollars in a designated slot in the door, and with a small pop it opened.

Stepping in, an automated voice said, "Welcome, where would you like to go."

"3249 Embarcadero." I replied, getting comfortable in the cheap plastic chairs. I looked up at the empty driver's seat. I never liked flying in air taxis, it felt weird with no one in control and leaving a machine to do all the work (and at that, especially a machine which had been designed so long ago). It was a short flight though; I was no longer stationed anywhere off base, so a thirty-minute flight was nothing.

The flight was silent, and it gave me time to relax from my hectic lifestyle. I stared out the window, watching my reflection in the glass skyscrapers which we flew right next too. I rested my hand on my chin, a gloomy expression on my face. For something I saw often, today the endless view of dark rock saddened me, the patch of green blocked from view just making matters worse. I could not bear to look one second longer at the horrible metropolis. Halfway through the flight I saw a building I had been longing to go into since my youth. *The Farm*, as it was called. In the center of the city, it looked like just another skyscraper except for the fact that it had no windows.

Maybe that was why when I saw it, I had to look away. It teased me, almost, what was on the other side of those walls was something I had rarely seen in my life. Plants. On every single one of its 240 floors there were rows and rows of greenery. Not just fruit and vegetables, but the Cortezeon plant. The giver of life. The outside atmosphere had become too toxic to grow anything that could be consumed, and so the plant life was locked away from unwanted human eyes. Just like the other Farms which were scattered across the globe, providing food for the ever-expanding population, and giving anyone with the right power a massive paycheck. If you wanted food, or to live for an amazing amount of time, then you'd have to pay.

Next to it, a group of protesters held their pickets high. They were protesting the Cortezeon Pill, unwilling to take it because they declared it had destroyed the world. They died centuries before anyone else. I never understand why they did this, and I might never. But some of them would kill those who disagreed with them, and though it seemed like the rebellion was fading, it was best to be careful. And how small they were from my height, though I could still see the dark blobs in the crowd who were officers. Breaking up the rebels with any force necessary.

When the taxi finally touched down right at the address I had asked to go to, I could not help but smile. With the Farm far behind me, and my son just seconds away, the sudden change in mood took me swiftly. My son would always have that effect on me, and he was the only thing that could. Stepping out, a thick ocean breeze hit my face, and I walked towards the building, not even looking back to watch the T-Flyer take off once more.

The building was enormous. Made from pure concrete unlike the other buildings which had glass, it went up for as far as the eye could see. The inside was not very nice either. The staff was mostly automated, yes, but besides that, everything was outdated. The blue carpet was dirty, and so were the curtains which covered the few windows. One of the elevators was out of commission, and the stairs... well, you didn't want to take the stairs. It was crowded too, but everything was. Of course, none of that mattered to me, what mattered was that I was going to see my son.

As I stepped into the one working elevator, which was covered in dirty clothes, I typed in a screen to go to floor 297. Instantly the elevator lurched, and very quickly, I started moving up. Floor one, floor two, floor three. Every second I went up a level, and with each floor gained, the knot in my stomach grew larger. I cherished every moment with Timmy, finding it to be a special time. Without his mother, he constantly stayed with my nanny, Mrs. Prescott. She was a soft old lady with glasses, and she walked around with a cane. Timmy didn't seem to mind, but I did. Not just because I never got to see him, but because Mrs. Prescott charged quite a lot just to sit at our house and steal my food. But if that was what it cost to make sure my son stayed safe, then so be it.

Finally, with a soft ding, the elevator stopped on the 297th floor. I stepped out, walked down the hall, took a deep breath, and entered room 11.

Instantly a small boy with my same blond hair, dressed in jeans and a red and white striped T-shirt jumped into my arms. "Dad!" Screamed Tim enthusiastically.

"Tim! How are you!"

"Great," he said, "Mrs. Prescott taught me how to knit!"

"Did she now?" I asked turning towards the old woman who was wearing a pink dress. "A five-year-old, knitting?"

"I wouldn't ask him to make anything though," replied the old woman already walking out of the room.

I looked around at my house. The floor was marbled and polished nicely, there was a couch in the center, where a large screen hung, a kitchen rarely used was placed in the back (even though it was well decorated), and there were two rooms on opposite ends of the house. I walked over to the large window at the other end of the room, looking down. You could barely see the bottom, and everyone looked so small. It was dizzying. From below everything seemed enormous, but from up here, it was all microscopic. All so bland, all so uneventful. I turned back to look at my boy, he was only four feet, but already at chest height. I was five feet. "So!" I smiled, "Any plans for the day!"

My son looked down to the ground, kicking it with his foot. "Well," he started, "I was thinking we could maybe go to the zoo."

I continued smiling, but at this point it was plastered on me. The zoo was incredibly expensive, costing as much as a month's paycheck. Everything cost so much, but on this one day when I saw Timmy... I collapsed onto the living room couch. "Now son, you know how expensive-"

"I know, I know Dad," interrupted Timmy, "it is just some of my friends were telling me how much fun it is and…"

Tim continued to stare down at the ground. I sighed. "You know what, why not!"

Tim squealed with excitement. "I'll go get dressed!"

"You do that."

As Timmy scurried off towards his room, I couldn't help but remember my last time at the zoo. Reminisce about my own time.

I had been around the same age as Tim, and though tickets had been less, my mother had saved up just enough money so I could go for my birthday. My mother had been a stubborn woman and had refused to take the Cortezeon Pill. She claimed that the world was better off before that foul drug. That it made us think we were better than everything around us. She had died at 87, an early age for the rest of the world, though she had died with no shame. I knew her as a good woman, and that day at the zoo truly showed her love.

I wanted Tim to remember me in a similar way. Yes, someone who wasn't always around, but still a parent who tried his best to show his son how much he loved him. Besides, I would have plenty of time to spend with Timmy later. He had yet to take the Cortezeon Pill, but when he did, we would be able to spend centuries together. I just needed to work now so we could spend time with each other later. That was what I always told myself.

Walking towards my own room at the opposite end of the apartment, the lifeless walls staring down at me, I began to realize that I too was excited about the zoo. Not just to create the same memories I had with my mom, but also just to see the animals. The creatures they kept in the small, dimly lit cages had not walked this planet outside of captivity for ages. Even the very few trees which you would occasionally see in the animals' habitats were rare. Unless of course you owned a farm, but most of those were just machine operated, and the farmer normally never saw his crop.

In my bedroom, a tight space with a twin tucked in the corner, and my wife's picture hanging everywhere, I went over to my closet. Searching through the very few shirts I owned that had nothing to do with the military, I eventually slipped on jeans and a large t-shirt, grabbing a sweatshirt from the ghostly white wall just as I left. Home no longer felt like home. And in fact, it never had. Not compared to the zoo at least.

There was something else about going to the zoo, seeing animals and plants. It triggered something in human DNA. Every person felt it. It was why zoos could charge however much they wanted. Even though everyone felt the same when they saw a plant for the first time, no one could name that feeling. Joy, happiness, pleasure. Or maybe it was just the warm feeling you got after returning to your house after a long day, the feeling when you knew you were safe, when you knew you were finally home.

..

I stood outside the massive sign for the zoo, which was painted green and spattered with bird droppings. Inside you could hear the calls of the wild animals and barely see the tops of trees which were just over the zoo barrier.

I always wondered why we didn't just duplicate what was left. We had that small portion of trees in cages, but we weren't allowed to clone or modify them *now*. Not since the ban on genetic sciences. However, if we could clone organisms, then maybe the world could be full of them again.

Timmy was holding my hand. He had changed into jeans and a blue shirt and had a soft backpack on his back.

"I can't wait!" He shouted, jumping and smiling enthusiastically.

I smiled back. "Neither can I!"

Tim ran to the entrance where families converged and began to buy tickets. "Hurry up Dad!" He shouted.

"I'm coming!" I yelled back, walking forward.

All around us were families, who like us were walking into the gates and getting tickets. But one family stood out. There was a mom, a dad, and a small boy in a stroller. The sight brought tears to my eyes, that was the family I had always wanted, and it would never be. What would life had been like if things were different? If maybe, just maybe, my wife had been spared...

"Sir? *Sir*?"

I snapped back into reality, and I realized I was already at the front of the ticket line, where a young woman was trying to talk to me.

"Oh, sorry."

"Sir, you need to pay now," said the woman rudely. She was dressed in a strange safari outfit, and she wore a large hat even though the sun was covered by the clouds.

"How much?" I asked sheepishly.

"$5,000 for both of you."

I cringed. That was more than I had expected. But then looking once more towards my son who was leaning through the gates, trying to catch a glimpse of the creatures which roamed inside, I couldn't say no. "Here you go," I said, taking out a wad of money from my pocket and not giving it a second thought.

"Have a good time," said the woman, waving us in and counting the money I had handed her.

Tim cut ahead of me and slipped through the turnstile; I followed, shouting at him to slow down.

Stepping into the zoo was an experience like no other. When you first walked in, trees and small shrubs lined the walkways, and farther off the path you could see small cages where animals slept and peered through the bars.

I found my son, staring into a dark, damp cage that held an orange-colored monkey. "It's called an orangutan, this sign says it's the only living one!" Timmy said, reading the worn-out sign before him.

I smiled at Tim's excitement as he watched the slow creature. Though I was just as excited as him, it was a sad sight. The animal just sat in its small cage, with no room to move. Occasionally it would pick at its orange fur, scratching its chin and looking back at us. "Hey dad, what's that weird thing in its cage?" asked Timmy.

Following my son's gaze, I saw that he was looking at the small fern that was tucked into the orangutan's habitat. "That's a tree son," it made me sad that my own child did not even know about something that once thrived on the Earth.

"I know *that*," said Tim, rolling his eyes at me. "They're all over this place. I was just wondering why the zoo wants so many of them. As far as I can tell they aren't doing anything."

"Well, they're an attraction, Tim. People come to see them."

"But they don't do anything!" Replied my son, throwing his arms up in the air.

I looked down at the young boy. It would be hard to explain something even I knew little about. When I was born, trees had been going extinct, and by the time Timmy was born, they had vanished off of the face of the earth. Removed so that a growing population could have homes.

It wasn't just that I didn't know about plants, I didn't even know how to be a father. I knew other dads probably had the same problem, but I was trying to parent a kid I rarely got to see. I sighed, I guess I would have to try my best. As I always did. "Well Tim, these plants are almost…almost like a…" I searched for the right word. "Like a treasure," I finally said, "These trees and even these animals aren't around anywhere else. People far in the past had them all over the place, but we don't. So, we must keep them locked up here. Safe."

Tim nodded with approval. "I still think they're boring though," he said.

I shook my head, he was young, there would be time to teach him the mistakes of the previous world. And looking around at the zoo, animals in cages too small for them. I wondered if the world had changed at all.

Chapter 2

I awoke with a fright. It was another cold, brisk day, and while I was getting dressed to see Tim again. I had gone home the night before to do some busy work at the institute but was now ready for another fun day with my son. I dared a peek outside hoping to see what I knew would never be there: green. Yet again, it was still dark and cloudy. Change is a challenging thing; you become so used to something that everything else seems awful. Yet the change I wished for, I knew would be a good one, and I hoped all of humanity thought the same.

Sliding out of the door, I jogged over to Janet's desk. "Checking out, I'm guessing," spat the old woman.

"Alright Janet, I want to get to my son so make it quick," I wagged my finger as I spoke.

"Oh Brian, I'm just messing with you. You're the only one here who actually talks to me. Now you go have fun with sweet Tim."

"Well, I hope you have a good day as-"

"*Lieutenant Brian Watson, please come to General Myers's office please, you are needed immediately.*" I turned to look at the loudspeaker mounted above my head, just as it screeched out the sentence.

Janet looked at me concerningly. "Sorry about that Brian," she said sincerely.

I couldn't stand the thought of seeing General Myer. He was the head of the institute and though I rarely saw him, people talked about him being insane. Of course, I didn't have anyone close to talk to. Most of the people who I had heard those words from had been fired. It also hurt that I had to cancel seeing Timmy. Timmy! I spun around just as I was leaving the large room, instinctively reaching for my cellphone.

I quickly dialed Mrs. Prescott's number, this was her day off, and I needed someone to watch Tim. She answered after a few seconds. "Hello?" Croaked the old woman.

"Hi, Mrs. Prescott this is Brian." I spoke.

"Ah, Brian, you know I can't watch Tim today, it's my day off."

Rolling my eyes and tapping my foot impatiently, I started to walk off to the general's office. What would Tim do without me, what could someone so young do in a world full of ancients. "I know, but this is really important, are you still at the apartment?"

"I was just about to leave," replied Mrs. Prescott. "I would love to watch him, but I'll need…"

There was a pause. I looked down, stopping in the middle of a crowd. "I'll do double."

"Great! That'll be $300. Have a good day Brian."

I hung up without replying, whatever General Myer wanted, it better be important. Every day it felt I had to pay more, every day I felt that I was giving Tim a bad life. It was all for my son, I had to keep reminding myself.

As I walked down the hall, I strode towards, and into the cafeteria where people were sitting down to eat and socialize. The closer I got, the more I could smell something salty and greasy cooking. If there was something I had learned in my 113 years of life, it was that American food had barely changed even though the country had been destroyed. It of course had gotten worse over time, fattening people up more and more over the years. Though they had made a drug for that, just like everything else. Just like age. Of course, there would always be somethings that could not be solved…

I continued walking down the hall and then turned right, where I assumed General Myer's office was. They had never really organized the Juan Cortezeon Military Institute, and as it had grown, the hallways had become more confusing. And it had grown a lot. Most people joined the military since very few other jobs were available. Just wanting to feed their family like me. So now it was huge.

The Institute had been built in Juan Cortezeon's honor. Juan had made the first Cortezeon Pill out of a jungle plant, and since research on the pill had needed to be done somewhere, they built the institute for studies. Eventually though, tensions in the world had risen, and it was decided for it to become a military base. I had been stationed at the facility my whole life, though would occasionally be shipped off for battle. The job had paid good when I first joined, they had given me plenty of time off, and I was close to home. What wasn't there to love?

This was no more though. I worked full days, sleeping at the base, always being ready if there was an attack. Hell, just last year the Rohans attacked Boston. And the year before that, Washington D.C. was almost hit by a nuclear warhead. Now, I was living paycheck to paycheck. Then again, so was the rest of the country. And though my job was no longer the best, there was no quitting, not if I didn't want to end up on the streets. With Timmy.

As I walked down the corridor, I kept looking at all the doors with names on them trying to find General Myer's room. Surprisingly at such an early hour the halls were already alive, and I struggled through the crowds. Everyone seemed excited, as if something big was coming. As if a storm was rolling in, electricity filling the halls. I also noted the number of new faces. It felt as if every day someone I knew was being sent out to battle one of the global superpowers only to never return. They were offered a promotion to entice them, and then the military shipped them out be killed. It was only a matter of time before the same happened to me. Eventually though, I came across a tinted door with: *Three Star General: Myer*, written across the top. This was only the second time I had ever been to his office, with him being so busy and all, he was rarely ever seen around the institute. The last time had not been particularly good. It was when he had told me I would have to stay at the Juan Cortezeon Military Institute and not go back to Tim who had just turned 6 at the time. That had forced me to get him a nanny 24/7 (save some weekends).

I pushed open the door, and there, sitting at his desk, and looking at his massive monitor, was General Myer. A tall, fit man with black hair that he had buzzed but covered by his dark green military cap. "Ahh, hello Lieutenant. Please sit down, sit down," the general said, not looking up from his work.

I sat down, nervous to speak. My feet, not touching the floor, kicked back and forth. "Um. You called for me General Myer?"

"Yes, I did. Now I'm going to be straight with you Brian. You weren't our first choice for this role. We have been taking heavy casualties and are running out of men. Your test scores aren't bad, so you're next on the list and…"

As General Myer continued to drone on, I couldn't help but note how all of this sounded, it felt as if he was stalling, burying something more important beneath a pile of words. But I spoke up anyways, interrupting the man. "What role are you offering me, general?"

General Myer sighed. "I'll get there, Lieutenant Watson. As you know, the Andy Region, and the rest of the world's goal has been to find habitable land," Myer began.

"We've ventured into the Amazon, and we are currently working to build housing, but we need more."

I nodded, still a little timid. "Yes sir, but everyone knows that we have found all the land to find. Correct?" I asked, recalling what I had learned from school when I was young:

The Andy Region controls everything. The Cortezeon Plant is money. Money is power. Power fuels innovation. To gain wealth, we must conquer anyone and anything around us. Anyone or anything who stands against our conquest is the enemy. Do not sympathize with the enemy. The enemy prevents you from getting money. Money is power…

And on and on it went. All lies. Everyone who had learned it knew it. Yet there was something about it, something about the way they taught those things to you.

They commanded the lessons onto you, and you *had* to believe them.

The general was speaking again. "Well, no, not exactly."

"What!" I gasped. No one had seen land not owned by anyone for at least a hundred years. Everything was inhabited, even the Antarctic.

"Recently, one of our expeditions sent this image." General Myer turned around his monitor, showing an image of a small rock jutting out of the sea. How small it was. Mere feet across. The sea splashed across it, wetting its jet-black rocks. Beneath it the giant creatures which now inhabited the dead sea swam around it, and vaguely, there seemed to be the outline of a door or some kind of man-made structure carved into the stone. "What's that?" I questioned.

The general looked at where I was pointing, then back at me, said, "I see nothing."

I ignored his odd answer, staring at the rock. Just this small piece of land was so much to me, the fact to see land that had not been changed by humans was extraordinary (even if it looked as if it had been). And though I was surprised by a part of uninhabited land, it was as if the general's only goal was to get there. And behind his power-hungry gaze I could see fear, as if there was something there that he wanted to hide from the world yet take for his own. What, I did not know.

"Why do we want it?" I questioned.

"We believe it will bring prosperity for the Andy's, just as the Farm system has boosted our economy." I rolled my eyes at this comment from the general, knowing that all high-ranking government officials supported the Farm because it gave them access to a huge monopoly. However,

General Myer continued, "This land has just been detected. Our satellites were unable to detect it because it was previously underwater. But with our new climate control measures, and thus a receding ocean, it had popped up from beneath the waves. And we have been looking for this *particular* island for a long time. It's right off the coast of another, larger island in Indonesia and we plan on getting it for undisclosed reasons."

I stared at General Myer. Something wasn't adding up. Why had they been looking for this island? What was there? "But sir, no disrespect, but it's still just a rock... right? What kind of prosperity can it bring us?" I asked, trying to dig for information. I still had no idea why anyone would want something so small. People want whatever they can get their hands on though, no matter the size. We are a greedy species.

"You'll find out if we are able to control it, but for now that information is classified. All I can tell you is what

I told you before. That if we *don't* take it, then our economy will fail," the general said, giving me a similar answer as he had before yet with just enough variation that I knew a little more.

"So, it has something to do with the Cortezeon plant?" I asked, remembering the nation's source of almost all income.

But General Myer just took a deep breath, then added, "It's code name is Dewa Ruci, an island three meters across by three meters, and only just above sea level."

I ignored his reaction, for now. "Dewa Ruci?"

"Yes, Dewa Ruci, the Javanese 'dwarf-god', and though it is small we wish to have it," General Myer snapped. "You have learned it is best not to be too nosy, have you not?"

I nodded quickly. "So, what would you like me to do General Myer?" I asked curiously.

"It is in my interest that you went to Stanford, correct?"

"Yes," I replied, failing to see the purpose of such a question. That had been years ago, before Timmy. But when I had just met my wife.

"Well then, I would like you, Lieutenant Watson, to become *Sergeant Watson*, and help lead a battalion into a fight that will hopefully allow us to take the island of Dewa Ruci," said the general, who was now calmly resting his palms in his lap.

I looked at him and was shocked. At that moment all the thoughts of the men before offered the same trap, thoughts of those who had died left me. Now, I was just grateful. I had been a foot soldier for so long, just another body the army threw towards a battle. So, I guess I sort of deserved it. *Earned* it, I told myself. But at the same time, I was scared. Not just for myself, but for Tim. I don't know what would happen if I died, and who Tim grow up with.

"General don't get me wrong; I'd love to help. It's just I have a son, and I don't know what he would do if something happened to me," I said sincerely.

"I understand Brian," scoffed General Myer, "but what If I told you that if you said yes, I could double, no, *triple* your pay!"

My eyes widened, thinking of the world I could make for my son with that money.

"I don't think I could say no to that general," I said laughing. The future I could create! All for my son. I even, for the time being, pushed the premonition that the general wasn't telling me everything out of my mind, too ecstatic to worry.

"Great, then it's a deal, Sergeant Watson." Then I shook his hand, praying that everything would work out. "Is that door closed behind you?" Spinning around, I saw that it was and nodded. "Good," the rough man replied with his southern accent. "Now, we must move quickly, so I will be showing you the plan right away." I saw General Myer reach his hand beneath his desk, and click, the wall beside Myer opened to reveal a holographic table. The sign of the wealthy. The hologram showed the Pacific Ocean, and in the middle was a small island. Dotted with trees and mountain ranges, fences, and beaches.

"What's this one?" I asked, pointing towards the big island in the middle, very much unlike the island the General had shown me previously.

"Hmm what? Oh, that's the Indonesian island, and that's Dewa Ruci," said the general, pointing towards a small black dot to the left corner which was barely visible. "Computer zoom in on plot 5G."

The hologram got closer to Dewa Ruci and began to give us a 360-degree view of it. I saw the doorway I had seen earlier but held my tongue.

Pleased by my silent response, the General moved on. "Computer," he said. "Move to location 7G."

The image rotated to the Indonesian island, which seemed a lot more significant than Dewa Ruci. It was covered with war defense and looked extremely menacing. In the ocean beside it was the small top of two ships. I nodded towards the island fearfully. "What are we going to do there?" I asked. "And what about those boats?"

"It's an Indonesian nuclear testing facility along as a home to some natives, though rumors are saying the Rohans and Tahoens may be getting involved. As for you, when we get there, an aircraft carrier will rendezvous with you and take a number of men to Dewa Ruci after you've cleared out anyone on the Indonesian island. Get rid of any enemies who stand in your way on the Indonesian base. It blocks the direct route to Dewa Ruci."

"And the boat?"

"That's not a ship at all. It's submarine, codenamed Bima. I will not go into the Javanese mythology behind that name, but the point is it is essential," said the general in reply.

"How essential?" I asked.

"Don't worry all will be explained. When we get to the island, we'll push the beach and go up the hill to set up base camp," General Myer spoke, moving *Bima* towards the beach by dragging the hologram.

"Sir, when you say beach—"

The general laughed, "I get that a lot. I've told others, and the rumors have been spreading like wildfire. Yes, beach, very little man-made architecture."

My mouth dropped, "Does that mean there's trees, and plants there!"

"Yes, in fact that Island is one of the few places left on this Earth, with a forest!"

Chapter 3

I looked into the grey, death colored water, wondering if anything could survive in it. Well, if anything natural could survive. Far offshore I could see the writhing of the giant mutated creatures which now controlled the oceans. As for anything miraculous in the sea... probably not, even to *smell* the ocean was awful. I had read that at one point the ocean was salty and smelled of it too. But the growing population had caused a need for salt, and so we had taken it from the water and dumped our trash in it as well. And as I looked into the water, I was overcome with a sense of woe.

The tide was low, and every day it was getting lower. That was, of course, because of the climate control measures. With global warming the sea had risen, covering most land for a couple of centuries. However, just recently a new system had been put into place which could control the Earth's conditions for the most part. It in truth didn't fix the world's problems, it just covered them up. Thus, is how problems are solved the human way.

I had already been waiting at the dock for a while. It was early in the morning, a dense fog covered the land, and offshore the sound of a distant buoy could be heard. Closer to the beach, the white caps of waves crashed against the filth covered beach. Yesterday, after showing me the war board, General Myer had told me to get up the next morning, bright and early at 4:00, and drive to the ocean.

Getting up had been the easy part, the shore was close, and the general had arranged a jeep to take me to the harbor. The hard part was when the driver had dropped me off a little too far away. And I was forced to step over homeless people (who were everywhere) just to get where I was standing now. Dodging them had proved to be a challenge. And had taken me most of the morning.

The dock was empty however, even though General Myer had told me to meet at this same time. He had been very vague though, about what the point of all this was. And the only thing on the dock was what looked like the top of a very small submarine. Nothing like the Bima the general had vaunted about.

It was also eerily quiet, and the city stank of gasoline and trash. Smog filled my lungs, making me cough of black phlegm. I prayed for Tim, who was much deeper in the rot, who was all alone. Turning my head back to the city, I tried to make out the skyscraper my son was in. Wondering how he had done yesterday with Mrs. Prescott, and if he missed me.

However, as I was looking through the thick atmosphere, the dot of green atop the hills and across the bay once more stole my attention. Taunting me. Begging me to go back and see it once more before I left. But I reminded myself that where I was going there might be much more than one or two trees. And in a way, that kept me waiting for General Myer.

When was he going to get here? It was toxic to stay out in such an atmosphere for too long. Then, I heard the motor of a vehicle getting closer and closer. And out of the fog came a dark green jeep. It reminded me of trees, and it caused me to smile, forgetting the sadness which had previously fallen upon me. The jeep stopped and out stepped General Myer. "Ahh, glad you could make it *Sergeant* Watson," the general exclaimed, elaborating on the word *sergeant* so I could remember what I had agreed to.

"Nice to see you today, sir," I said nervously.

"It will be nice once we have Dewa Ruci. So, ready to start your first battle as a sergeant?"

I still didn't know how I felt about him, or how I felt to have my position as sergeant. To be honest, all I could think about was my son. And though I couldn't put my finger on it, I could sense he wasn't telling me something, "Yes sir," I lied.

"Great, then we're ready to go aboard," General Myer said excitedly.

Without waiting for me, Myer started walking towards the small submarine. As I stepped closer to it, stepping onto the wet ramp which rattled beneath my feet and led to the small submarine, my anticipation and fear started growing.

I wanted so strongly to get paid to help Tim and see what the general had kept so secretive. Tim needed the best life, no matter what. My fear on the other hand, which overwhelmed every other emotion in me, was horrible. What would happen to Timmy if something happened to me? Where was I going, this couldn't be the Bima, could it? As I walked up the ramp, General Myer turned around and must have seen my face because he then asked, "I know how you're feeling son. You're scared to disappoint your country, aren't you?"

I stared at the general, wondering what the man was thinking. General Myer did not know how I felt. In fact, lately, I had been questioning my faith in the Andy's. When the people of the A.R. had been in trouble, the government had looked the other way. When people were dying, they looked away. When I needed help, they looked away. And if people like General Myer were in charge, I didn't know if I wanted to be in the same society as anyone like him. But because he was my superior, because of Tim, because of the fact that I had been conditioned in such a way to love my country with all my heart, I lied. "Of course, the Andy Region has given me so much, it is time I repay them. Like I always have."

The general nodded at my words in approval. "You'll do just fine," he said. "And if you're ready to go aboard, I would like to introduce you to the captain, of this vessel. Please meet Captain Johnathan Herbert!" And at that moment the general stepped away from the hatch he was blocking, to reveal an old man with a white beard and a white uniform. In fact, I couldn't tell where his beard ended, and his suit started. He was also smoking a pipe, which smelled strongly of tobacco. I was sure you could smell it from miles around. His age was hard to tell, but I estimated it at about 200. A good, solid age. But almost the end of his long life.

As I wrinkled my nose at the captain's pipe, he looked at me, almost pondering what to make of me. "So, this is Sergeant Watson?" the old man asked. He cast a look at Myer. "You're sure he's a good choice for this particular...."

"I'm sure."

"Well then, welcome aboard Mr. Watson," Captain Herbert said, grabbing my hand and shaking it firmly. "The general has told me much about you. Says he asked you many things to make sure you were the right choice. However, I have my own questions." The old man took a step towards me, eyeing me.

"Fire away," I said shakily.

"How many wars have you fought in?"

"Three," I replied.

Captain Herbert asked, "Your combat record?"

"Twelve dozen enemies killed, served in two sperate battalions."

The captain seemed pleased with this and stepped back. "One more question then. You have been serving for some time; you have enough money to take care of yourself…"

"Is there a question behind all this, sir?' I asked interjecting.

Captain Herbert ignored me. 'Why do you keep fighting?"

Without hesitation, I replied, "For my son. I am a father, and he is too young to take care of himself. I do it all for him."

And it was true, that was why I fought.

Captain Herbert smiled and began to move on. "Well than, ready to step on to this mighty vessel." He gestured to the minuscule, bobbing submarine behind himself.

"Is that the *Bima*?" I asked the captain.

"Bima is more of a name we like to use with… civilians. But yes, this is the Bima. Or the H.M.S. Franciscan, as the crew calls her."

The captain opened the creaking hatch, and I stepped into the submarine. Ecstatic for what I might see.

But what I saw was almost nothing. The room which I had walked into was one of the most boring things in the world, which is saying a lot for someone who lived in a place so full of people, and concrete buildings which hid most things from the eye. The inside of the Franciscan had one flickering, unnatural light at the top, and had only one interesting thing about it. A spiraling staircase, that seemed to go on forever into the darkness of the lower decks. And as I peeked over the edge, the captain noticed my curiosity. "This ship gets a lot more complex. We just built this part to confuse intruders. Follow me," Captain Herbert said, beginning to step towards the stairs.

As I followed Johnathan Herbert down the winding staircase, groping in the dimly lit ship below, I wondered if this was a clever idea. I had seen no one else close to where the H.M.S. Franciscan was, and I knew little about the ship as well. You always had to be hesitant in this modern world. Mercenary groups were everywhere, prowling the Earth and looking to take out their next victims. They were like the rebels I had seen from the T-Flyer in the sense that they wouldn't take the Cortezeon Pill, and they protested against our governments. Except that their form of protest was much different than most of the rebels. They attempted to kill anyone who *did* take the Cortezeon Pill, claiming that by minimizing the population they were helping the Earth. Or at least that was what the A.R. told us.

I kept walking, however. Because if I kept walking, I could get paid more, and if I could get paid more, I could give my child a better life. Which is every father's one goal. The further I went down though, the more I started to question my decision to come on this mission. If it was worth the risk.

Though soon enough, the darkness started to fade, and a soft glow of light began to take its place. With every step down on the slippery stairs the light grew. All until soon, I stepped out into something glorious, and worthy of an amazing title. "Well, here she is, the Franciscan at her best!" Spoke Captain Herbert loudly, standing taller and straighter than before.

"Yea, isn't she something Watson my boy!" General Myer said.

I didn't know what to say, my mouth was wide open. The ship was hard to put into words; the size itself was immense. Though I knew it was a submarine, and yes, submarines are big, this one was on another scale. It went on for almost as far as I could see, and had dozens of floors, each one with people bustling around off to do their jobs. At what seemed to be the bottom of the sub was a wide-open area with computers scattered around and people typing and speaking into headsets. It was truly awe inspiring. As I looked down though, I noticed something odd. Towards the bow there was a stage with a podium set up on the front, the A.R.'s flag unfurled above it with patriotic pride.

"She is something. As big as the Empire State Building and capable of housing 30 nuclear submarines. All you saw was the very top. We actually had to deepen and widen the docks just so it would fit. And not to brag, but the president is even on this ship and will be giving a speech later on our voyage," said the captain of the miraculous vessel I was on, blowing on his pipe and cracking a smile as he spoke.

"Wait, President Kyle is here?" I asked surprised.

"Yes, he insisted he be here to motivate everyone in this time of hardship," said General Myer.

Time of hardship? Had this not been a simple task? Had I not signed up to just lead a team into a small battle? What was so special about this island? Or was nothing special about that island in the middle of the ocean? Maybe this conquest for land had gotten into people's heads. And people like Myer had gone insane with the hope of expanding their empire. But not President Kyle, I reminded myself. He was different. There had to be good reason for him giving a speech.

I just smiled and nodded, hoping President Kyle would explain our need for this attack. The general and the captain then walked me down another flight of stairs to where all the computers were, wanting to show me where most things happened on the vessel. "This is the belly of the beast Brian," spoke Captain Herbert. "Most advanced system on the planet!"

We continued to stride down the aisle ways which separated the computers from each other. The men and women working at them were focused on work, but occasionally one or two would stick up a hand and wave to the captain in a friendly gesture. Soon we stopped at one of the many screens, where a woman sat and worked on the glowing screen. She had perfectly tan skin, along with amazingly green eyes that popped against her long blonde hair. She also wore a standard ships uniform. When he approached her, she stood up and saluted Captain Herbert and the general. "This is Lieutenant Susan Winter. She was a great help in finding Dewa Ruci," said the captain.

"Nice to meet you," I said.

Susan put her hand down and nodded towards me smiling. She was a pretty woman, about my age, and seemed nice as well as oddly familiar. Like some ghost from the past, or photograph that told a forgotten story. Either way, I thought I recognized her from somewhere. "You as well Mr.…."

"Watson. Sergeant Brian Watson."

"Oh," Susan laughed. "You probably don't remember me, but I believe we were in advanced biology in college."

I studied her more closely, and then I remembered. Susan had been the most popular girl in school. Everyone wanted to be with her. I… well, we had almost been a thing. But then I had met my wife, and well… "No, I remember you. I don't know how I could forget. You were studying to be a doctor, correct?" I spoke.

"Yes," she smiled. "And you were doing biology just for fun. With Kate. By the way, how is she? Last I remember, you and her were about to settle down and start a family. You would always talk about it in class, telling me how happy you were to raise a kid. If I am honest, I was a little jealous. So, is she doing well?"

"She… she passed away not too long ago." I replied a little shaken.

Susan closed her mouth and looked at General Myer after that.

"Well, you two better catch up. Brian, Susan will be part of your battalion, so I suggest you learn her strong suits and such. Like I have said, we don't have much time." said General Myer.

"Yes, ahh, General Myer I'd like to talk more to you about the ship, let's leave these two to reminisce alone. Also, Brian, would you mind meeting me at 1900 hours on the fourth floor?" asked the captain. "I'd like to show you to your room, and if we have time, allow you to meet the rest of your squad."

"Sure."

As the two men walked away, I was left with Susan. "So…" said Susan, leaning against the desk which held the computer, "you're the sergeant?"

"Yea, I'm as surprised as you are. Never expected to get this far."

"Neither did I. As you already know, I had dreams. I started out in maintenance here though. Somehow got promoted," she shrugged, "life's a mystery." I nodded in response. "Hey, you want to go get something to eat or drink, they have got beer. None of its good, or alcoholic, but it's the only beer on the ship," said Susan.

"Alright, let's go," I said awkwardly, bouncing on the heels of my feet.

I followed Susan throughout the ship. Winding through passages and stairs which formed a maze out of the titanic submarine. Getting the occasional glimpse of some wonderous sight that made my mind spark with questions that I desperately wanted to know the answer to. I thought of the people above, of the one hold of greenery left. How I longed to see it. Eventually though, we arrived at the cafeteria, sitting down at a plastic table. Susan asked, "You know what this *mission* is about?"

I shook my head. "I'm just doing it for the paycheck. Got to keep up somehow."

Susan laughed; it was pretty, like sweet music. "I hear that."

We sat there for a while, drinking, laughing, having a good time. We got into more personal issues though, sad topics. I told her about my life. How Kate had died, and I almost never got to see my son. She felt sympathetic, holding my hand as I explained. She then explained her life. She had graduated from Stanford with her PhD however had quit the medical profession when the XG-971 virus hit.

Those were rough years. The virus was a genetically modified version of Coronavirus. Created in a lab as a type of experience. A bioengineering experiment. The virus had gotten out though and caused a lot of problems. The symptoms were nauseating, and the survival rate was 0.1%. Many people got it too, because of course, everyone was so close to each other that it spread easily. A cure had been created before anything could get out of hand thankfully, and nothing like it would ever happen again, because after that, the whole world had decided to not only ban genetic science, but destroy any work, or people, related to it. Thus no one knew anything about that ancient profession.

Now, years later, she worked in the military, one of the only jobs you could get nowadays, trying to take her mind off those horrid days.

But we also talked about school. We both remembered getting to know each other in that crowded university, and the friends we had made along the way. She already knew about my family, so I asked about hers. She said her parents had been killed in a riot, by rebels, and surprisingly, she didn't seem too mad. I wanted to ask how Susan felt about the rebellion, but we were getting along

73

well, and I didn't want to ruin the moment. It still felt strange talking to her though, knowing what we could have been.

I looked down at my standard military watch after some time of conversation. It was 1830 hours. We had been talking for so long! "Oh my God! I have to go. Sorry," I said sincerely.

"No problem. Maybe we can get another beer sometime," said Susan, fidgeting with the glass in her hands.

I blushed; my cheeks becoming warm. "Sure, I said. See you later!"

Then I was off. Running as fast as I could towards floor four. I ran up the stairs faster than lightning, arriving right on time behind General Myer and Captain Herbert who had their backs turned to me. I was panting. They turned around to see me mid conversation. "Ah, sergeant, perfect," said the General. "We should get going again. Captain Herbert, will you be coming?"

The captain looked down at his wristwatch. "Well, Myer it's getting late so I must go up to the bow now. We're about to depart. Oh, and would you mind taking Mr. Watson to his room, it's going to be a long day tomorrow," said Captain Herbert, already walking down the corridor of the vessel.

"Well," said the general, rubbing his hands together, "Let me show you to where you will be staying. I am sorry we didn't have the time to meet the rest of your battalion, but we can do that another day."

As I followed General Myer down one of the submarine's many halls, I saw the black water outside had begun to get even darker. Seeing the void only made me more exhausted, making my eyes sag with sleep. I couldn't help but imagine living down here for months. It must be miserable, never seeing the sun. Then again, that was the world I lived in. Total darkness, separated from every other human being.

Nonetheless, my eyes were beginning to sag, and each step I took felt like walking through thick mud. The general soon turned to me and asked, "This may seem odd, but did you happen to know Charolette Hive? Personally, that is. She did go to Standford with you, did she not?"

I looked at him closely and could tell he seemed skittish. It had been a long time since I had last seen Charolette… it had been college. Just like Susan. "Yes," I said, wondering what General Myer's plans were.

Myer just nodded though and said, "I'd start thinking about her more."

Eventually we turned down a new hall that had a sign above it that read, *Barracks 3329*. How many people were down here?

"Right here my good man," said General Myer turning his body, and spreading his arm to give me a view of the small room with a bunk bed and a sink. "It isn't much, but it will do. Oh, and dinner will be delivered shortly, you must be starving. I doubt you ate breakfast, and we didn't have any time to eat lunch."

"Thank you, general."

"Ah, no big deal, anything for a fellow Andy leading his troops to battle. You know I used to be like you. Helping fight for the great Andy Region. And besides, we can't have soldiers dying of hunger, now can we," replied General Myer already walking down the hallway.

This would be interesting. I stepped into the room, my feet clacking loudly on the hard tile. I tried sitting down on the bottom bunk but bonked my head on the cold metal. That was going to leave a mark. And I had to wonder who was going to be staying with me, because I could tell they were packing the submarine to maximum capacity. Whoever it was though, they were probably too busy with all that was going on, for they never appeared.

Later that night, my food was delivered, it looked to be tomato soup and a piece of moldy bread. But I ate, too hungry to complain. And as did, I heard the captain come on the intercom and say that we were leaving the port. I had not seen the intercom before because it was so small, which I guess just showed how advanced the ship I was on was. I looked down into the red, watery dish while wondering where this submarine would take me, and my future.

Probably nowhere much, I guessed. I mean, we were just fighting for a rock, nothing more. With that I put my food down, slipped into the rough sheets of my bed, letting my heavy eyes rest, and my tired feet as well. It felt good to sit down, I liked days like these. Where nothing seemed to matter, and after a long day you could rest. I hoped more days like the one I was experiencing were

ahead of me.

Chapter 4

We had gone 2,000 nautical miles west when I awoke. 2,000 miles farther away from Tim. The night before, I had dreamt that on a small beach I had been shot, the military didn't send my family anything I had earned, and there was no one to help or love Timmy. My responsibility ever since Kate died. He had mourned and ended up on the streets. Only to die alone, as I had.

I shook that thought away the moment my eyes opened. That could never happen, I was stronger, I would not die. And even if I did, Tim was even stronger, he would endure. Right? As I slowly got out of bed and brushed off my uniform which I had been too tired to take off the night before, and, standing up, felt my hunger and started to wonder what was for breakfast. Just before I walked out the door though, I did what I always do, look, and freshen up my hair in the shattered mirror of my room. And then, I was off. Down the hall and following whatever sign I could to the cafeteria.

There was no smell to warn me what we were having for breakfast, since it was plain vanilla yogurt in a prepackaged cup. Inf act, it didn't even have any granola or any other topping. Just the prepackaged filth. However, I stayed optimistic, thinking that maybe it was not that bad. There were people starving, and the military would take care of us. They had to. When I went up to get my food, the exhausted looking cafeteria worker, with her drooping eyes, her head resting on her hand, and a sagging hairnet, just looked at me perplexed. As if I was some unknown species. She pointed towards a bin of yogurt and said, "Serve yourself."

I got my breakfast, along with a spoon, and then started looking for a drink. The cafeteria woman said, "If you're looking for a beverage there is a water fountain on the next floor down."

"Thank you," I said, quickly looking away and rolling my eyes. Yet I attempted to remind myself to be grateful, remembering that my conditions could be much worse.

Obviously, even if this place was advanced, their food wasn't, and neither was their care of soldiers. Eventually I finally found the water fountain. I had already eaten my food, which was definitely spoiled, but while I was drinking the cold, rusty water, out of the corner of my eye I saw General Myer walking down the hall. Surprisingly not in his usual military uniform, but in a tightly groomed, three-piece black suit. "Hello sir," I said trying not to stare, and standing up while water dripped from my chin.

"Well hello sergeant, are you coming to the President's speech?" General Myer asked.

"That's now?" I asked surprised, for a split-second pondering why the general had not told me, but soon realizing there were probably more important things to think about.

"Why of course, it's already eleven in the morning!"

"Is that why you're dressed so nice?" I asked, starting to stretch and shake the remaining sleep from my body.

"Got to look sharp. This is all so important, and since I'm leading the event, I want the president to know I'm doing a good job. Anyways, the speech is on the tenth floor, just follow the signs if you want to come," The general said.

"Thanks, I think I will," I said, the excitement of seeing the president building inside of me.

"See you there then. Oh, and if you do come, it will be a good time to tell you where you'll be meeting your battalion."

I was going back down to get more water when he said this and nearly choked. I was surprised, though I knew I would have to meet my soldiers soon, it startled me. In fact, I was still getting used to the fact that I was a leader, and no longer just your average soldier. I was about to ask the general if I could meet my squad now, having built up the courage, but the man was already backing up, showing how anxious he was to meet President Kyle.

After my general was gone, I started to follow the hallway he had taken but eventually came to a fork in the road and had to look for signs to help me get to where I needed to go. Thankfully, I didn't need to. You'd think the performance of the ages was happening. As I got closer to the tenth floor, more and more flyers started appearing. They showed President Kyle standing up straight and tall, and staring off into the distance. They made him look like a god. And soon, part of me had even begun to think he was.

Eventually though I arrived at the bottom of the H.M.S. Franciscan. The tenth floor. Around the big stage which I had seen when I had first walked in, there were chairs that had been set up overnight. Several Andy Region flags lined the side of the stage, a circle with two black stripes crossing right through it. The lights were now shining onto the podium, casting a halo onto Kyles printed head which covered the stage.

As I walked into the core of the ship, I started looking for a place to sit. In the crowd of people starting to fill the many chairs spread around the podium, almost every seat was filled. Everyone had come to worship.

Out of the corner of my eye, as I was looking for a spot, I saw General Myer. Slightly embarrassed, I was forced to sit with him when he waved me over. I sat down in the white plastic chair. For a while we sat in silence, watching as more and more people flooded the halls. People. A species which ruled the Earth and believed in equal rights for all. Yet not everyone was equal. Finally, after some time went by, General Myer spoke up, saying, "Want to come with me to see President Kyle? Herbert asked me if I wanted to come over and see him, and since you're one of my favorite soldiers," the general grabbed my back as he said this, "I thought you should come. I mean, we both just want to serve this one man, so might as well meet him."

I didn't know what to say, see the president! Though I feared the general, I wanted to see if the president's views on this… Dewa Ruci were as intense. If this was a conflict which I should be scared to participate in, or if it was one I that would be quick and easy. "I… I… I'd be honored, sir," I said in reply faltering.

"Great, follow me then!" Said General Myer.

As me and the general got out of our seats, it felt like my heart was leaping from my chest. I was scared of one man. Even though that man was *helping* me. I still couldn't help but think though, what if he wasn't helping me? What if he was just helping himself? Taking advantage of a world full of people, making his empire larger, and putting everyone at risk while he did so. Selling us a drug that seemed like a miracle and yet was a curse upon the globe. I had seen something on that image of Dewa Ruci. Something I felt that others, not just President Kyle, would use against the good of humanity. But no, I *had* to trust our government. I repeated the chant to myself:

The Andy Region controls everything. The Cortezeon Plant is money. Money is power. Power fuels innovation. To gain wealth, we must conquer anyone and anything around us. Anyone or anything who stands against our conquest is the enemy. Do not sympathize with the enemy. The enemy prevents you from getting money.

Money is power…

But as I walked behind the stage where General Myer was leading me, the pit of fear in my stomach started to grow. He was the greats of the greats, he was the leader of leaders, he was… and then I saw him, President Kyle.

Chapter 5

When me and General Myer turned the corner around the stage set up for the president, we saw him talking to Captain Herbert and seemed not to like what the captain was saying. "What do you mean 'spotted something on the radar', Herbert?! I need answers, the fate of this vessel's crew lies in-" the president of the Andy Region stopped in the middle of his sentence when he noticed the two of us. "-oh hello, Mr. Myer," he said nervously. "Captain Herbert told me I might be able to see you today. Always an honor to meet one of my military's most prestigious leaders."

"The honor is mine Mr. President, sir," said Myer bowing low as if meeting a *king*.

"Ah, and who is this young gentleman?" Said President Kyle turning towards me with his soft hands behind his back, a smile on his perfected face.

The president was an odd-looking man. He had brown hair, which was parted to the left, making him look younger. Though if you looked at his hands and face, you could see wrinkles, only proving his age. He also had a young smile, and extremely white teeth. Interestingly the only normal thing about the man was his size, six feet, the average height. He towered over me. Though, maybe he had just forgotten to change that part about himself.

Lately, it had seemed like everyone wanted to change a part of themselves. To stick out and be unique. In a crowd of people, it was hard to get attention and to be wanted. To be loved.

Snapping back to reality I replied to the president's question. "I'm Sergeant Brian Watson sir; I'll be leading a battalion to storm the beach next to this 'Dewa Ruci' everyone is talking about."

He pondered what I had said for a moment, eyeing me up and down like I was important. Like my part in this mission was more than it seemed, like I played a part. Then, after he seemed satisfied, President Kyle said, "Excellent, nice to meet you Mr. Watson, and I hope you lead your battalion well. If there even is a battalion left to lead!" while looking back at the captain. "And General Myer, this is *the* Brian Watson you were telling me about?"

I looked back at my general wondering what the president was talking about, but he just shrugged. More secrets, more hidden information that only those who were *worthy* could have access to.

"Anyway, good luck Sergeant Watson if we are to take Dewa Ruci, we must take the small Indonesian island next to it. It has certain defenses that can keep anyone away from the prize. And if we can't take Dewa Ruci, then all is lost," said President Kyle, pounding a closed fist into his hand, messing up his perfect hair as he did.

Well, that answered one of my many questions. President Kyle was just like the general. Wanting nothing but Dewa Ruci and whatever it held. Dead set on wealth or whatever other secrets the island hid from view; corrupt. For most people that wealth came from the Cortezeon Plant. Using it and others to achieve their goal. People were like that, that's why I tried my best to space myself from them. Even if it was a lonely life.

I was still clueless as to what was on Dewa Ruci, but I knew it was hiding something that the president sought. Something that was worth going to war over. Something that justified sacrificing people's lives.

On the edge of my vision, behind the president, I could see Captain Herbert roll his eyes and turn away. I wondered then how the captain felt about Dewa Ruci. He probably just wanted to get paid and get out. Just like me. And did he know? Know why we were doing all this?

Such complicated times. Then again, generation after generation had thought the same thing. Our lives were just one screwed up mess in a long line of others. A short blip in time.

"Well," the president said straightening the nice blue suit he was in and glancing at his watch, "it's... showtime!" And with that he walked out of the curtain and got a roaring round of applause as he stepped up to the podium. They adored him. Adored him for his journey for wealth and power, and whatever it was he wanted.

Wanting to see the action, me, General Myer, and Captain Herbert all started walking back to the seating area to get a better view. And as we walked the captain slowed down, saying. "I know how you feel."

I tried to look at the captain, confused by what he was saying, but he grabbed my shoulder and said, "Don't look, it will draw attention."

Staring dead ahead, my eyes were focused onto the back of General Myer, who was just about to sit down. Captain Herbert guided me to a dark corner of the ship as the general did this. He pulled me against the metal hull. Still not knowing what was going on, Herbert continued in his low whisper. "You don't know why you're here, do you?"

I shook my head.

"You don't know what is on Dewa Ruci?"

"No," I muttered. My throat felt like it was closing up.

Captain Herbert looked around to see if anyone was looking and then leaned even closer to me. "Nothing is as it seems," he said. He let that sink in for a couple of seconds. "Why do you think we *all* want Dewa Ruci?"

"All?" I rasped.

The captain nodded. "The A.R. isn't the only country after what is on that cursed island. We aren't just about to fight a bunch of natives on an island."

"Is there a problem here?" Asked one of the president's personal guards who had worked his way over to us, looking at myself, then the captain, and then back to me.

We both glanced up at the towering woman, shivering, not knowing what to do.

"Not at all sir, but we will be taking our seats now," replied Captain Herbert.

We walked out skittishly to our seats; the fluorescent lights of the submarine started to dim as we did. Darkening until an eternal black encompassed all. Soon, the only lights left were the ones coming from the spotlights, all of which were directed towards the lectern. There, a banner was draped that had the A.R. symbol on it. A dark shade of green, even if the rest of the planet wasn't, as if representing what we everyone wanted. Reminding me of that small Eden on the horizon which tempted me. Behind all of it was President Kyle. After some time, the only other light was the dim glow from the outside sun, shining through the port holes of the ship. But we were too deep to get much of it. And above the waves, clouds blocked it out, like they always did.

We sat down and waited for the president to begin. I kept finding myself looking back at Captain Herbert. What was on that rock? What had I gotten myself into?

President Kyle cleared his throat. "Hello, my loyal military. As your 13th president, it is my duty to inspire you all with greatness…" he said, leaning on the podium and looking down at his pre-written speech. "…so that on the battlefield you are about to face, you may have, and feel courage!" I looked around at the other members of my country. Most were dressed fancy, but some, like me, were also in their military uniforms. All though, had their chins raised high, and looked proud to be an Andy, proud to be here. It was magical, a light of hope shining off the president almost. It didn't matter what he said, they just were glad he said it.

I remembered the great battles of the ancient past I had learned about in school. One of which was when our first president, and the founder of the Andy Region, Oliver Murray, had led his troops to victory. Men had charged into battle to overtake the corrupt countries which had treated them horribly. That same rebellion would pave the way for the largest superpower the world has ever known, the A.R. Or at least, that was what we had been taught.

I wondered if Oliver had inspired his troops like Kyle was doing now. And if his troops had felt the way I was feeling now: patriotic, courageous, and like they could face the world even though they were so small. All those feelings and dreams drowning out that since of logic I had just recently felt. When just moments ago I had been pondering about what secrets the government had been keeping from me, now I was following them blindly.

As President Kyle kept talking, the more these feelings grew inside of me, making me feel large and big. The more I listened to the president's every word. And every time noise came out of his mouth, the more I forgot about what it was me and the captain had been discussing. "Every day you have lived on this Earth," President Kyle said, "has led you to this moment. A moment when you will serve your country in battle and earn your name in the history books. The upcoming days will be some of the greatest in the world's history. Generations upon generations in the future will remember the brave men and women today, that saved our country!" The president shook his hands in the air, getting a cheer out of the crowd. "Your children and grandchildren will look upon you in wonder as you tell them the story of this day. It will be tough out there, but we are tougher! The foolish man is the one who quits dreaming because he finds it pointless. The wise man however turns that dream into a goal, and though he may not make it all the way, he will always get close! He gains wealth, and wealth is what?"

"Power!" We all screamed in unison (even Captain Herbert). We were all in a hypnotic trance.

"But a man can dream all he wants about his goal in life. It is those who work hard that complete that goal. Those people go down in history. So, which will we be?! Will we be those who go nowhere in life, because they do not put in the effort? Or will we be those who put in the work and accomplish what they truly desire. This is what the A.R. stands for! Which will it be?!?"

"We will put in the effort!!" Screamed the crowd, courage their fuel.

I was in awe. In awe at how just one man, could inspire a whole army. Most of us did not want to be where we were, including me. I would rather be at home with my son than here, or at the Juan Cortezeon Institute for God's sake. President Kyle's speech though, had inspired me so much. So much that I was proud to be where I was. Even though I had no idea why I was here, and that mystery had been previously eating away at me.

But then I saw the president's eyes. So filled with that fire that could be seen in General Myer's eyes. That hungering, envious stare. They were the same people, President Kyle and the General, both feeding off of the people they controlled, the people who gave them money to live forever. There was something on that Dewa Ruci which both men wanted, on the other side of the door I had seen which may have not been a door. Then, in one instant, I was snapped out of my trance, and my mind began working functionally again.

At that moment, I was so incredibly conflicted. I wanted so badly to create that perfect world for Timmy, but it didn't feel right helping someone like the general. Someone so bent on making a fortune off others and maybe destroying the planet as they did.

I then remembered the rebels of *my* time, and the active rebellion which was happening as President Kyle spoke. They didn't care about living forever. They had given up everything because they saw what the government was doing. Just another thing for me to think about.

As the president went on with his speech, the crowd's hearts filled, and the army's motivation to win was felt. The talk went on all day, and General Myer, along with other guest speakers, went up on stage to give their opinions. However, each one stumbled and the real energy was of course felt during President Kyle's remarks. But soon, everyone seemed to start getting tired. And by midday, even President Kyle, who had been very enthusiastic at the beginning of his speech, had started to calm down and slow. So in that way, the president finished his speech with, "We must win!"

And as the crowd started clapping, I looked around the H.M.S. Franciscan. At those men and women who I was proud to fight alongside. Even if just for a short period, and even if my loyalty was slowly shifting. Of course, the only person that did not look proud about the current situation was Captain Herbert. Who I had noticed had been frowning the whole speech, especially now. Even more curiously, once the clapping had slowed, the captain heard his walkie-talkie go off and put his ear to it. That's when his frown turned into something that would have made you think someone had died.

After saying a quick word into his radio, and putting it back to his leather belt, the captain slowly started walking up the stage straight to the president. The audience went silent as Captain Herbert ran up; his steps echoed throughout the hall. When he finally got to him, and all eyes were staring, unblinking, he came so close to President Kyle's ear that his white whiskers were touching it. Just as the captain's frown had deepened, the president's deepened as well. Kyle's eyes widened, and he seemed ready to exclaim a thousand curses.

I looked over at General Myer, hoping he would know what was going on, but the general was just staring out of one of the port holes. Thinking Myer was just daydreaming, I ignored him, but I soon realized he had a look of terror on his face. So great it made my own heart stop.

I glanced into the water, seeing nothing. But when I looked more deeply into the grey, dark ocean, I noticed there was a shape. A large shape. It was round, almost oval. At first, I thought it was just a smudge on the glass. That was until a streak of bubbles flew out of its front. They looked red and hot; it was heading right for our vessel. It went straight towards the bow, and when it hit the ship, the whole thing shook. Sending me lurching forward, and other people right out of their seats. That was when I realized what had been seen on the captain's radar.

Chapter 6

The explosion put a ringing in my ear, and I was blinded by a blinding light for a moment. Almost far off, I could hear Captain Herbert shout into his walkie-talkie. "Close the blast door, now. And get me a damage report. And for God's sake fire back at that submarine!"

The chaos around me was immense, as folding chairs fell, and people screamed, and ran around to do whatever they could to help, I stood still in shock, watching as two large men in black suits slowly escorted the president off the stage. They left once they had him. No one was coming for us, the Andy flag lay tattered on the floor, being trampled. I shook the terror off though, and instantly the soldier in me kicked in. I immediately turned to General Myer who was barking orders at men around him, trying to resolve the destruction. "Anything I can do to help sir?!" I asked screaming over the disarray.

For a second the general seemed not to heed my words, struck by the chaos as I had been. Then he replied, "Yes, go find Johnathan! He'll be doing a lot; you best go help him!" And then General Myer was back to yelling at his soldiers.

"But isn't he right here…" I said, turning back to the stage. No one was there.

I looked around, searching for the old man, but he was gone. I looked for someone, anyone, finding a young man, not much younger than myself, who seemed, like the rest of us, to be in deep shock. He seemed more frightened than anyone else though and was clenching onto one of the few white folding chairs still standing as the vessel rocked. So afraid of death, a strange thing if you never died. As I approached him, his eyes turned to me, and he stood up strait in a salute. "Hello sir, anything I can do, sir," said the young man.

Not used to being respected as that, I paused for a moment, remembering that I was a sergeant. How powerful I felt then. I didn't know how he could see my ranking in the dark though. Actually, the submarine had darkened even further since the blast armor had been lowered onto the port holes, excluding all light from the outside. "Umm... yes. Yes, there actually is," I said, attempting to test my strength, and how far it would take me.

"Anything sir!" Said the boy, still saluting me.

"I need to know where the bridge is," I replied. "Any idea?"

"Alright, you're going to want to go down that hall over there, take a left to get to the stairs. Go to floor zero. You got that zero!" He said looking me in the eyes and pointing towards the hall he was talking about. I nodded. The boy continued, "Good, then go right, and there should be a hallway which will lead you directly to the bridge. All good?"

"Yes!" And then I was off, jogging down towards the corridor the boy had talked about. All the while muttering the instructions he had given me, repeating them without hinderance. I didn't care who I was helping, or even if I still had my doubts about Dewa Ruci, I just needed to do something. To help. That was how I worked. And it would be better if more people worked that way too.

After turning left to get to the stairs, as the young man had instructed, and making sure to go to floor zero, the task of getting to the bridge was fairly easy. I just ran off to the right. No time to slow, people's lives were at stake.

As I sped down the many hallways towards the bridge, where I hoped the captain would be, on the way seeing many people like me. Jogging, and running frantically. Only stopping when the ship would list or shudder. What everyone had hoped would have been an inspiring, hopeful day had turned out to be a day that was horrifying and dangerous. I felt dazed by the sudden excitement. As if I had just woken up from a long nap and was now watching as screaming men and women cried out and died. I was in the thick of battle already.

At one point, a woman came up to me begging for help. I wanted to aid her so badly. To help get the dust, soot, and blood off her face. But something inside of me, some instinct, told me to keep going. That I needed to complete my job. Not wanting to be cruel though, I looked around and found a soldier who seemed less occupied and asked her to take the woman immediately to the medical station.

After that though, every single person I saw, anyone who was hurt, I longed to help. I didn't though. I couldn't. Something told me the captain needed me more. I felt like a monster leaving so many injured people just lying unattended to. And yet I knew I had to keep pushing on. It was weird that not only me, but others, didn't even notice the people that were injured. They just ran by. That had to say something about the planet's condition.

By the time I reached the bridge and opened the plain, black door that led into it, my chest was pounding. I put my hands on my knees, trying to calm my heaving breath. But I had no time to rest.

"Ah, good, Mr. Watson, I need your help!" I looked over to see Captain Herbert hunched over a monitor screen, towards the left of the room. Which surprisingly was empty. "Hold this please," said the captain tossing me his pipe, which was as black as the room we were in, having probably been blowing it through his stress.

I also noticed Captain Herbert had rolled up his white sleeves and was sweating quite profusely. As I looked around the dark room, the only light was coming from the screens set up around the bridge. Some of which were broken, others dirty, and the rare few perfectly fine. The windows to the outside were sealed with the blast doors, causing me to notice how quiet the room was. It was an eerie quiet too, the kind of quiet which told you that you were alone. An almost screaming silence I was not used to.

"Captain Hebert, where is everyone…" I started to ask.

"No time to explain boy, head over to that screen over there. The door to the torpedo room is jammed by fallen debris. Our men down there can't fire back at the enemy if we don't clear it!"

I trudged through the frigid water, my legs feeling as if daggers were in them. Why was there water in the ship? I then looked forward, and realized that before the blast doors closed, there must have been glass up there. "Hey captain, what is with all the water?" I asked, trying to clarify my assumption, and take my mind off the fear inside me.

"When that torpedo hit, it broke all the glass that made up the viewing area. When that happened, water rushed in. Killed everyone in here," Captain Herbert said with a sigh.

"Killed people?" I looked down into the dark water. Except it wasn't dark. Upon looking closer, I realized the water had the faintest touch of red in it. "Blood," I mouthed. Looking closer at the room, my eyes adjusting to the dark, I noticed that spread across the room were bodies. Floating face side up, and down in the water, were bodies. Bloody, gory bodies. Each one, unmoving, cold, and wet. They floated on the surface of the water and when the submarine shifted, they would drift with the current.

Though I had seen corpses before, for God's sakes I was a foot soldier, this was different. Before I had been fighting for a patriotic cause, a cause I cared about. But this, this was a strange new feeling. I did not want to be here; I did not have that burning patriotic fire in me. I was scared. And I was sure the men and women whose bodies I was looking at, had probably felt the same. These people could have had families. Yes, I could imagine it now. Some government official coming to that person's family and breaking the news. In that moment I fully realized, if I died, my son would have to endure the same experience of these soldiers' families. Though I would be gone, it would not be me who was in pain. It would be my little boy. Having barely known his own father and being shipped off to an orphanage.

And as I looked down into that water, floating with people who had families, I realized, this fight was not one I wanted to be a part of. I didn't care what was on Dewa Ruci, I needed to get out of here.

Slowly, I made my way to the control desk. Still trembling from the shock, and fear I was in. "Wha-wha-what do you want me to do n-no-now sir?" I asked, my voice shaking.

"Go into the home page, and you should see a big model of the Franciscan. It should have some labels throughout it. Find the one that says *Weapons Holding/Firing*. Click it, and it should zoom you in. When it does, you should see what looks to be a large robotic arm."

"What is it really?" I asked, trying to take my mind off the horror of which I had witnessed.

"A large robotic arm. What did you think?"

"Nothing, nothing," I said, a lump forming in my throat.

Out of the corner of my eye, I saw Captain Herbert looking at me. He continued what he was doing but started speaking. Sweating over his work while trying to coax me. "Look, son, I've seen countless men die, and… oh what am I talking about. You have seen battles before, that can't be it," said the wise, tough captain. I saw him look closer at me. Up and down. Pondering my motions and expression. Then as if something had clicked in his brain he said. "Son, death is a part of life. No matter how immortal we think we are, no matter how invincible, we are all going to die," he laughed. "Some sooner than others. For just trying to explain Dewa Ruci to you as I had moments ago, I will be killed.

I became anxious. "But why?" I asked. "Tell me what is on that island!"

The captain just kept on smiling. "In truth, I barely know! You'll have to find that out for yourself. And does it really matter? For millennia there have been times when people have been forced to do things they don't want to do. Things that may kill them…" I then thought he was about to tell me to toughen up, but he instead said this: "Though, when that happens, us, as a small insignificant species, rise up, and fight for what we think is right. Now tell me. Does this feel right to you? And if it doesn't, you should start asking yourself: what can I do to make a difference? That is how you will find out about Dewa Ruci. Because if we didn't stand up and fight, this country would not even be here today. I agree with you, son. What is happening is not right, I know that is what you think. But you need to buy your time and wait until you can do something useful. There are people on this ship that may agree with us, agree that this conquest for that tiny island is not right, and if you don't help to save them… they will die. Never getting a chance to do anything," finished Captain Herbert.

I looked down, thought only for a split second, and instantly turned back to finish working on the computer.

I couldn't let people get hurt, especially if they were like me. Fighting for something just to keep afloat and giving everything to a society they might not support. They fought anyways though. Like me, they needed to. I would find a way to make a difference however, somehow…

"Excellent! Now when you click on the robotic arm, controls should pop up…"

"Um, Captain, sorry to interrupt, but why hasn't that submarine destroyed us yet?" I asked curiously. Focusing back on my mission.

"I said our weapons systems were down I never said this baby was defenseless," said Captain Herbert, slapping the ship with his hand. "Once they fired, an automatic stunner kicked in! Disabled their main cannons for the time being," The captain peered into my eyes. "Feeling better?"

"Yea, now let's get rid of them, before they get rid of us!" I said, a glimmer of hope starting to shine in me.

"That's the spirit! Now once with the controls, simply use them to pry open the hatch, I'll try to coordinate with the men downstairs on what to do," said Captain Herbert turning back to his own screen.

I looked back at my own black and white camera view, which showed me what the arm saw. I slowly, cautiously pried the cover to the missile loading dock open. It wasn't just that I wanted to make a difference, I also couldn't run. Not wouldn't but couldn't. The dead men on the floor had not run. And they had not wanted to be here either, I was sure of that. But they knew it was their duty to serve their country, and that's what they had done. That was what I would do, for now at least.

Finally, after wrestling with a piece of wedged metal deep within the ship, a loud scraping sound screamed from the computer screen, and the broken hatch pried open. On the other side of the computer, I could hear men cheering. But as all this happened, it occurred to me what I had just done. I had made it possible to kill all the other people on the other submarine. Sure, they fired first. Sure, they were the enemy. But what if some of those people were like me, what if they had not chosen to be where they were. Herbert had said it himself, there were people like us who didn't deserve to die. What if they were forced into what they had done. As these thoughts flew through my head, I started to ask the captain what he thought. "Sir, is it really a good idea to—"

But it was too late, as the words left my mouth, Captain Herbert clicked some buttons, said some words into his walk-talkie, and at last, hit a big, red, flashing button.

I watched through the cameras. Following a flash of light from beneath the ship, a stream of bubbles shot forward as the torpedo left the vessel. And as the camera angle switched, I saw the enemy submarine, defenseless, and unmoving, being shot at. The projectile touched the vessel, I saw a light brighter than the sun, and I knew there would be no survivors. I knew I had just help kill thousands.

Chapter 7

I awoke from my uncomfortable bunk bed, with the creaking of the ship. The night previous I had one of the worst dreams. I had walked on a desolate, barren land, crater filled and dark. All around were corpses, bleeding and dead. I knew it was my fault. And the worst part was, I knew this dream hadn't been very far from the truth. I *had* killed people, *many* people. All with the press of a button. All in one night.

As I stretched my aching muscles, I looked up at the ceiling. Trying not to cry, trying not to explode in a fit of rage. However, I was surprised to see two bare feet dangling from the bunk above me. Looking up, I made a creaking sound from moving on the metal bars, and the person occupying the top bunk looked down and spoke. "Oh! You're finally awake!"

The man looking at me had red hair, very tan skin, and was extremely fit. A perfect person, some would argue. He looked oddly familiar to my tired eyes. I tried to wipe away my tears.

"H-hello. I'm—"

I was embraced in a massive bear hug before I could finish speaking. "Brian!" Screamed the man, good to see you!"

I blinked the sleep from my eyes, trying to understand what was happening. When I could finally see clearly, I realized I was looking right into my good friend Charlie's face. I began jumping up and down excitedly, holding the man in front of me. I knew I had a huge smile on my face. "Charlie Richer!"

"Brian Watson. Or should I say sergeant?" Spoke my friend with his deep raspy voice, still holding my shoulder with his massive hand.

"How do you know?" I asked.

He smiled. "Well, I'm in your battalion." Charlie let go of me and sat down on his bed.

I stared into those brown pits of eyes Charlie had, the eyes that seemed to mix with his hair. The eyes and hair of my friend, my only friend.

Charlie had lived in the institute like me, and we had connected well, he had even known my wife. And before that he had gone to Stanford with me. But all that had changed when he had been shipped off to war like so many others. And though being reunited with Charlie should be joyous, knowing he was in my battalion sickened me. I couldn't lead; couldn't lead someone into a situation they may never come out of. Why though, was I leading another college friend?

But I sat down next to him, trying not to think of the worst-case scenario. The bed creaked under the extra weight. "How'd you make it here?"

Charlie smiled again, that big, bright smile that would never leave his face. "Was fighting some Rohans off the coast of New York, got called up here to deal with this Dewa Ruci. Now, I'm working on maintenance. Had to deal with that sub we got attacked by yesterday, I've been working since we first got on this ship, not a moment to rest." I nodded. Charlie asked, "How's Tim?"

I chuckled, thinking of my boy, I said, "Tim's good, why do you think I'm here."

"Nice," replied Charlie. "I always liked that kid."

We sat in silence while we both woke up a little more. That just gave me more time to ask questions. Me, Susan, and Charlie. All from the same college, all on the same mission, all on the same battalion. The general had mentioned Charolette Hive, who had also gone to Standford with us. Was she part of this ever-thickening plot? I would ask Susan and Charlie when I had them both together. Though it had been a while since I had last seen them, I felt very connected to the both of them. As if they were that complete family I had always wished was my own.

Charlie broke the silence. "Oh yea, General Myer told me to tell you that later today you got to meet the rest of the battalion."

I gulped. "Today?"

"Today."

Charlie punched me playfully in the shoulder. "Don't worry, it won't be a big deal. But for now, I have some more maintenance to work on. You can come if you like. We got hit really bad in the hull. Might be pretty nasty."

I shrugged. "Sure," I said.

"Great, but I need breakfast first, I'm starving."

We walked off to the cafeteria, talking about the good times we used to have together, and reconnecting over the small boxes of cereal we each received. Charlie was able to sneak two, and we both laughed at how the cafeteria worker had failed to notice. It was good. Good to be back with a friend, that is. Charlie used to watch Tim for me when I was on the bases, so he had always been a big help. But also, it had just been nice to have someone to talk to. I didn't mention that though, I just wanted to laugh with an old companion. And try not to think of the battle ahead. It still felt strange leading a person I had always thought of as my superior. So, we talked about the vessel we stood upon.

"So," I started, "how much damage did we take?"

In between his big bights of food, Charlie spoke, "Well, I haven't seen any of it yet, but it's supposed to be bad"

"Are we alright?" I asked.

"Yea. The general showed me some blueprints of the Franciscan. This thing is a tank, can survive anything."

I thought for a moment. "If we have all of this," I waved my hands around, "then why are we after one small rock in a world full of wonders and amazing things."

"I don't know."

"You don't think something is suspicious?"

"No."

"And another thing," I said, "Do you think it's just coincidence we got put in the same battalion along with-"

He interrupted me when I was about to mention Susan, shrugging to silence me, just wanting to choke down the rest of his meal.

At that point I stopped trying to pry. We had stepped into an elevator and Charlie had pushed the button labeled *-60*. So down and down we went, and as me and Charlie rode the elevator further and further into the belly of the beast, we both stood quietly, the hum of the electric machine was all we heard. Charlie had always been a great guy but had never been someone known to question our government much. But that was most of the world and *had* been me. Still was me. At one point it went completely silent, and the elevator stopped with a lurch. I fell forward, drawing blood on one of the handrails. I had sliced open my chin. Charlie helped me up. "Powers out at this part of the ship. We'll have to walk the rest of the way."

Charlie took the top off from the elevator and then hoisted me up. I gripped onto the damp metal where water dripped down from the ceiling far above me. "Take my hand," I yelled down into the machine. Charlie reached out and grabbed me with his hard, dry palm. I pulled him up.

"There should be a maintenance hatch somewhere. We'll have to go through it if we want to have any chance at fixing…" Charlie waved his hand around where there were wires crackling, and water spilled from holes in the ship, "all of this."

I nodded. "Where to?"

Charlie proceeded to walk me in and out of a series of chambers, eventually stepping out of a cramped tunnel into a room flooded waist deep with water. It continued, jutting through a gaping hole in the dark. Charlie and I both flicked on our flashlights, illuminating the room in streams of white light. There, a man stood finicking with a panel of electric wiring. The man had dark skin and dark black hair. He also wore green pants and a green jacket, both of which were soaked chest height with water. He had a large build, similar to Charlie's, and when he heard us sloshing through the water, he looked up from his work. "Charlie? Good, just in time. Get over here will you!" He was shouting over the roaring torrent that spilled gallons upon gallons of water on top of us.

"Coming!" Charlie said, trudging over to the man, "Brian you come too!"

I half swam half walked through the water. It was frightening, my breathing was becoming faster, and I kept staring down into the liquid, fearing what it contained. I shined my flashlight where the man worked. "Darry, this is Brian Watson, my sergeant and good friend. I brought him down to help. Thought a little excitement could be fun."

Darry eyed me. "Charlie, I think this is a little bit more than a little excitement. Brian, I'm sorry he dragged you into this. I've been down here since last night and I've barely survived. Ever since that torpedo hit, the water has been rising, the electrical is on the fritz, and the nuclear reactor might just explode!"

I raised my eyebrows, too shocked to speak for a moment. "I thought you said this place was indestructible!" I yelled at Charlie. He shrugged. "Can't we just drain the water?" I asked.

"That is exactly what I am trying to do. This water is partly sea water, but mostly the water that cools the nuclear reactor that powers this vessel."

"So, this water was coolant for... doesn't that make it radioactive?"

Darry frowned. "Yes. Again, I have no idea why Charlie brought you down here. Big idiot."

"How do you plan on draining it Darry?" asked Charlie, ignoring the fact he had been insulted once more.

"The ship was built with a failsafe, if anything hits the core then it will cut itself off from the rest of the ship. It will just float away. We have a backup so it's no big deal. Right now, I'm trying to see if I can drain this water into the backup core. If I can do that it will detach itself because it will sense an outside entity. Right now, it is just extra weight though, and since General Myer wants us to go as fast as possible, he wants us to lose it. Two birds with one stone. I should be..." A light started flashing, and a smile hit Darry's face. "There we go! Fixed! Didn't even need your help, Charlie!"

Charlie turned to smile back, and then his face went white. As if he had seen a ghost. I followed his gaze into the darkness and saw that the hole we had exited to get into the cavern was closing. Darry ran towards it cursing. "No! No!" He slammed into the wall just as a hatch covered the hole. Darry put his hands in his knees. Charlie had a stricken expression on his face.

"What's the matter?" I asked confused.

Darry pointed towards the water line. "The water will start rising even more now, that was the only opening where we can get back to the surface, and the only place where the water was draining."

"Can't you just reset it on the panel? Or pry it open?"

Darry was still keeled over. "The water has risen already and fried the panel, and the water pressure is sealing this thing tight. At this rate we'll drown before anybody knows where we are."

Charlie still looked upset, but also as if he was thinking, pondering what to do. I was thinking too. Would I die here? Drowning for a cause I had yet to understand? All of a sudden Charlie exclaimed, "Darry, couldn't we use the maintenance hatch above?"

Darry popped up, pondering what the large man had said. "We could, but neither of us   could fit," as he said this, he caught my gaze through the gloom. "But *he* could! Brian, you see that crawl space up there?"

"Yea," I replied. It was nestled between some hanging wires and the wall on the other side of the room.

"If you can get up there you should be able to access another room."

I looked at the hatch fearfully, though I did not show it, I was very claustrophobic. I nodded; sighed. "I'll do it."

"Ok, get up there. Hurry!"

I started the climb when the water was already chest deep. We didn't have much time. My breathing was quick and heavy from the moist air. Every sound I made echoed throughout the hull of the submarine. I slowly pulled myself onto different boxes and footholds, making care not to touch any of the live wires.

Occasionally my hand or foot would slip on the slick surface, and I would grasp for air but then keep moving. I didn't have a choice. Charlie would yell up with phrases of encouragement, and it felt good to have someone rooting for me. I had missed having a friend. Even if Charlie was ignorant, we had known each other for so long, and I didn't really have anyone else.

I finally made it to the metal hatch, with cuts and bruises on my body. It was remarkably similar to an air vent, and unfortunately the same size as one too. "Alright take the cover off and start crawling through. I'll contact you through your radio. Channel three," said Darry.

I clutched my radio and then proceeded to crawl through the cramped vent. Water dripped from the ceiling, and I was squinting in the darkness, trying to find my way in the creaking vessel. An eerie quiet filled the air, nothing but the drip of the water and the occasional bang of something falling far off was heard. The drip of water. *Plink! Drip! Plop!* It was maddening. Though so small, it was amplified by the tunnels. Darry came onto the walkie talkie. "Brian, can you hear me?"

"I can hear you," I replied jittery.

"Ok, coming up turn left into the tunnel. Then hug the right of the vent for the rest of the way."

"Ok."

Groping in the darkness, touching the walls to figure out where I was, my flashlight having run out of batteries already, I ran my hands on the slick walls. At one point I felt something sharp cut my hand, felt blood drip to the floor. I remembered how the water was radioactive and what could also smell the blood in the water. It was a strange world; you could never be too cautious. Soon, a light began to shine from ahead of me. A light? Wasn't the power down?

As I crawled closer and closer, the horrible smell of burning gas filled the air. I knew what it was, even from so far away. Everyone alive could recognize the smell. It was too familiar. The government had taken gas and burned the national parks, burned farms, burned anything which was taking up land so that skyscrapers could be built. Things like churches or even just homes were destroyed. All apartments now. It was gas, burning gas. And the fact that I instantly knew the smell, proved just how strange the world had become… but every generation thought that. We were just one small people that had lived in one small, strange period.

I spoke into my walkie. "Bad news, there's a gasoline leak in here or something. Whole rooms on fire."

Darry cursed on the other end, and then I heard some arguing between Charlie and him. After a brief moment of me sitting in the tunnel, breathing in the smoke. Charlie came on. "I hate to do this to you, but you must go in Brian. The waters up to our necks."

Smiling I said, "Was never planning on going back."

I popped out into the burning room. The flames dancing on top of the water, licking my legs occasionally. The oil wouldn't get on me though; all the clothing I wore was military adapted. Especially made to make sure oil wouldn't seep into the fabric. That didn't mean I couldn't be burned though.

I waded through the oil slicks towards a control panel that I saw on the other side of the brightly lit room. The flames seared my skin. Thankfully the water here wasn't as high. I grabbed onto it, prying it open. The burning metal charred my bare fingers. Inside there were a series of buttons and switches which surprisingly had power, most likely backup. "Charlie, I made it into the control panel," I said.

There was a short pause and then Charlie said, "There should be a switch at the top labeled: *Prime*... pull it."

Pulling the switch my fingers were seared once more by the incredible heat. An electric hum then filled the room. "All right, now what?" The flames were becoming larger and closer to me. The heat making me sweat and my skin boil. I wiped perspiration from my brow, I needed to get out of here soon.

"There is a button at the bottom, push it."

Pushing the button, the electric hum became louder. Again, though on the other side of the walkie-talkie I heard both men talking in panicked voices. Charlie came back on. "Brian, run!"

"Why?" I asked confused.

"You're in the part of the reactor that's going to separate. Now get back here!"

I turned back towards the tunnel I had exited. It was closing! I ran towards it, not caring that the flames burned my skin, or that I tripped in and fell in the oily water. I jumped into the closing hatch, but I was too late. It closed on me, and I banged my head against it. I came up gasping for breath. "Charlie," I panted, "it closed! The vent closed," I coughed.

Darry came back on. "Son, I'm sorry, there's nothing we can do! Even if we open that hatch then the whole ship would flood when your side slips into the sea. We would all die! There is nothing we can do…" The radio once more slipped into argument, and then static.

The water started swirling beneath me. I knew

Darry was right. Every soldier was prepared for this. The

ultimate sacrifice. It was an honor, it was just that right

now, for this country, I didn't want to die. Not here, not

now. Not when I had just gotten my friend back. Not when

I still had so much to learn. I heard a banging on the hatch;

I thought it was the reactor detaching. I prepared for my

death. The banging continued, and then surprisingly, the

hatch pried open, and Charlie stuck his head in. "Charlie?"

I asked surprised.

"Come on let's go!" Yelled Charlie, he grabbed my

hand and pulled me in with him. The hatch fell, and we

were jumbled together in the darkness.

"What were you doing? The whole ship could have

been lost!"

"Yea but you know, I couldn't lose my friend. I

don't have anyone close to me, and… we have to stick

together." He replied, allowing for me to crawl in front of me.

Smiling, I said, "Thanks."

We crawled back through the tunnel, absolutely dumbfounded. My heart pounding, I turned back to see Charlie close behind me. I could hear the reactor core detaching. I didn't know why Charlie had come back for me, and as I kept going, I realized something. Darry didn't want to help, risk his life for just one person; I doubted the General would have, or even President Kyle. But Charlie did, because he was a good person, because I was a human being. Not just that I was his friend or a fellow Andy, but because I was human. You rarely see people like him.

Why did people become what they were today? Was it the plant? Was it the plant which had caused us to fight for Dewa Ruci? Something told me I was on the right track, but that the plant was more linked to that island than I could imagine.

Me and Charlie jumped down into the now receding water which was only ankle deep. The lights were back on, and I could fully see how destroyed the room was. Darry had a frown on his face. "You shouldn't have done that Charlie; you could have killed us all!"

"Charlie was just trying to-" I started.

"Stop," Darry said sternly, interrupting me, "Charlie you best go on. What you did was foolish, Brian was ready to make a sacrifice for his country, a great honor. The Andy Region would have labeled him as a hero, and you *took that away from him.* Go now, before I decide to report you."

Charlie and I rode the elevator up in silence. Charlie looked depressed, and I could tell that he and Darry were friends, and it must be hard to lose someone like that. But beneath that frown I could tell he didn't regret anything. He had made a decision to save an old friend, to do something loyal. To be a good person.

Finally, after some time had gone by, I asked, "Where are we going, Charlie?"

"To meet the rest of your team, it's already time," he grunted. I was surprised, time had flown, and I didn't know if I was ready. I drummed my feet on the floor beneath me, trying to get the butterflies out of my stomach.

Charlie frowned when the elevator stopped. "Come on, let's go."

I followed Charlie down towards where President Kyle had given his speech just last night. The night before. It did not feel like the night before, it felt like another world entirely. Charlie still seemed upset, so I tried to make small talk and make sure my buddy was alright. "Hey, do you know what happened to President Kyle?" I asked curiously.

"My friend is one of his bodyguards," said Charlie, waving me off, "he's fine. Though they took him straight to an escape pod. Just in case."

Walking further and further into the massive ship, I started to think about the president's actions. Men had willingly sacrificed themselves for Kyle, and this country. *I had almost sacrificed myself!* And yet the president had been about to just walk away! And as my thoughts drifted, the more I pondered it, the more I started to realize how corrupt this country was. Thinking about the general, the president, and how they had been treating us… it left a bad taste in my mouth. Yet, I knew I was not just fighting for the Andy Region, I was fighting for a better future for my family. Though somehow, I knew that more money, a bigger house, none of it would satisfy me. There was something I longed for, though I did not know what it was, I knew I wanted it.

Eventually, me and Charlie made it to briefing room 46, an ordinary-looking room, with the same style as the rest of the H.M.S. Franciscan.

Opening the door into the briefing room was like stepping into another world. While before, the rest of the ship and been lit with bright white light, this room was very dim, the only light was coming from a hologram map in the center of the room, which had flashing lights and buttons, all of which beeped annoyingly. Spread around the chamber, standing, sitting, watching screens were at least two dozen people. When we stepped in, they all stood up, and cheered. Hooting and hollering for me and Charlie. For me. For saving the ship. I was embarrassed at first but eventually found that the cheers were music to my ears. I was happy to be finally recognized; it gave me a sense of superiority over my comrades.

But the applause stopped, and Charlie sulked off, still upset. I now stood by myself in a sea of people. Some came up to pat me on the back, but most just got back to work. In a way, it reminded me of the real world. So many people, and I was so alone. I looked excitedly around the room for Susan, who I knew was here with the rest of my battalion. I caught a glimpse of her, and I thought she smiled at me but then someone came up to talk to her, and she got distracted. She was right behind a table which glowed and sat in the center of the room, standing and talking to the person which stole her attention. Looking closer though, I realized it was General Myer himself. The general saw me and ran over. "Hello Sergeant Watson, I hope you have had a good day on this vessel. And I must thank you for helping to fix our reactors." His eyes drifted to Charlie who was on the other side of the room, probably informed about his behavior. "But we got to move fast, the Tahoens attacked San Francisco last night. Thankfully we stopped them."

My eyes widened; rage filled my vanes. Didn't he know that countless lives had almost been lost?!? The Tahoens, like the Rohans and the A.R., were major world superpowers. The Tahoens took up most of Europe, the Rohans controlled Asia, Australia, and half of Antarctica, and the Andy Region had the rest of Antarctica as well as the Americas. You couldn't just act like the Tahoens attacking a highly populated city was nothing!

So, I had to wonder, why was he like this? Was the power he had handled the culprit which had made him a monster? Was he chasing Dewa Ruci for the same reason, power? Was that power behind the door which I had seen on that image of Dewa Ruci, but which the general had tried to hide from me. What game was this evil man playing? Finally, no longer able to contain my rage, I yelled, "My son is in San Francisco!"

"No matter sergeant, everything is ok. The situation is under control." General Myer laughed. "I would have been more sympathetic if I had known your son was there, sorry."

I calmed down, taking deep breaths. "Any casualties?" I asked.

"No, of course not!"

"Good."

"But sergeant, before we meet your battalion, would mind if we have a small talk?"

Uneager to meet my crew, I replied, "Sure, if you'd like."

He stepped over to two chairs seated at the holographic map. We both sat down, and General Myer sighed and then began speaking, "We are aware of the situation that occurred today-"

"Do not blame Charlie!" I screamed.

The general put his hands in the air. "I would have never dreamed of such thing." He stopped, thinking for a moment, and then continued by saying, "But I do have some things I would like to know that are related to Mr. Richer, as well as yourself. You have already confirmed with me that you knew Charlotte Hive…" So back to this again! Another college peer, and an important one at that! What was his angle? Every word General Myer said only raised my suspicions of him. "… however, I would like to know how personally you knew her."

I thought for a moment, remembering ingenious, strange woman. "We were close," I said.

The general smiled. "What can you tell us about her?"

So suspicious! She definitely played a large part in these Dewa Ruci charades. But how? "She is a highly unpredictable person. When you think she is going left, she is going right. Unless of course she knows that you know she is going left. She is always one step ahead." The general nodded at my highly complex statement. "Now general, I must ask this: is Miss. Hive attempting to capture Dewa Ruci as well?"

"That's classified."

. . .

Walking with me down the aisles of screens General Myer began showing me my men. And when I walked with him, all eyes seemed to follow me with a sense of thanks and pride. One person even saluted me, and it felt good to be recognized for something. Eventually though, I was introduced to a young man, talking into a headset, who was blonde, freckled, and very skinny. "Mr. Watson, I'd like to introduce you to Darlin McGinnis," said the general.

Darlin was busy at work and was silent. I really wished Charlie was here. He wouldn't have a problem talking to this quiet, boring stranger. So, I was on my own, with Mr. Darlin McGinnis. "Nice to meet you, I'm Sergeant Watson, I'm going to be leading you," I said.

The man swiped his fingers across the screen, and talked lightly into his headset, and then nodded softly. I rolled my eyes. "So... what department are you in?"

"Computer analysis, technician, anything that involves computers," said Darlin, not looking up from his screen. "I help with setting up radios in battle most of the time though. Occasionally fight."

"Ah, well, there's more of your battalion I'd like you to meet. Anyway, bye Darlin. Have fun with whatever you're doing," said General Myer, trying to get away from the peculiar, Mr. McGinnis. Yet however strange it sounded; there was something I liked about Darlin. He didn't seem like the usual people you found in the world. People who were cruel and evil. Darlin seemed nice, and I felt that if given the choice to save me like Charlie had done, he would have chosen to save me.

That day, we met multiple men and women. Some of whom were lieutenants, radio operators, medics, and many others. A few stood out, like when we met a man named Thomas James, a medic. When I walked over, he was patching up a man without an arm like it was nothing. He seemed fairly pleased about the war we were in. I met a woman, a foot solider like me. She didn't talk much, was too focused on fixing a gun, and she gladly thanked me for what I had done with the reactor, and I felt a warmth spread through me, knowing I had helped.

Towards the end of the day, when me and General Myer were both very tired, the general introduced me to a large, muscular man, somehow larger than Charlie. "And finally," started General Myer tiredly, "this is Lieutenant Sam Tyler." And at this point, the general was already

153

starting to fall asleep on his own hand while leaning on a battle board.

"Hello Mr.-" I spoke.

"No, just Sam, nothing fancy. No Mr.," said Sam waving me off.

"Oh, ok. So, Sam, what do you do?" I asked. Looking closer at the thick man who towered over me, I noticed a couple of things. First of all, he had many tattoos, running up and down his thick arms, and clearly visible because of his sleeveless shirt. And along with the tattoos were the scars. Scars from bullet wounds and knives. He was a fighter, and a good one at that. Highly intimidating, and his pitch-black hair only made things worse. I wondered why he wasn't leading me. In fact, I wondered why I was leading anyone in the room I was in. I shouldn't be in the possession I was in, that was the thought that kept running through my mind. "Me?" Sam asked, laughing and loading a machine gun, so big no one else could carry it but him, "I just shoot who I'm paid to shoot!"

So, another one. Another person who didn't care about human life. I had met people like him so much throughout the day that it was beginning to hurt. Seeing him made me glad there were people like Darlin. Glad there were people like Charlie that would save a man if they could. Glad that maybe the world wasn't all evil.

Chapter 8

The large man before me continued polishing his weapon, unfocused on myself who was microscopic compared to him. I was so... unnecessary.

The general didn't care about me; I knew that now more than ever. He just needed information about Charolette. He didn't care about my questions. Of how I wanted to know how dangerous this mission was. He didn't care that I had a son, and that I wanted to know if I would get back to him. For the longest time the government had taught us their founding principles. The A.R. promoted the fact they wanted us to make money and to gain power. But in fact, those were the things they were trying to keep away from us. They were the only ones getting rich, with their Cortezeon Plant, and the horrid Farm System. It was not right! The common man got nothing in return for years of service to his country except a pat on the back. It was not right!

However, I suppressed my rage for the time being. Still, I thought about what I could do. What if I could fight back? Fight for what I thought was a correct way to treat other people's lives?

Looking at my battalion, I was pleased though that these were the people I was going to lead. But as I was feeling proud, and happy. I was soon brought down by a sound that made my heart stop. *"All active troops, get to your battle stations. All active troops, get to your battle stations,"* blared the robotic speaker, with a siren going off in the background.

With the startling sound blaring, all the people in the room jumped to their feet, rushing out the door. Even General Myer awoke from a nap on the battle board, dazed and confused, but soon found his feet. "General Myer, where do we go?!" I asked, shouting above the noise.

"Sorry, I didn't have time to brief you, just follow your battalion! Good luck!"

My eyes widened and I stared at the general. "Already though?" I asked.

"Yep! This baby can haul!" Replied General Myer, he too, already running out the door.

With the alarm still screaming in the background, I looked around for Charlie and Susan. Thankfully, Charlie was jutting out of the crowd, and it was hard to miss, however I couldn't find Susan. "Well, you ready Mr. Watson?" asked Charlie smiling.

"No, is anyone ever ready for something like this?" I asked, looking down at my boots, and frowning.

"No, probably not. But sometimes it's these events that shape us into the people we're meant to be. Though we may never be fully prepared, sometimes, there is no way around it," said Charlie aspiringly, starting to pick up speed with me, and following the rest of the men down a long flight of stairs.

"Yea, well, I had no preparation at all." I replied.

"Oh, well. I don't think anyone did," Charlie said. "But at least we get to fight together."

For the rest of the way down damp stairs into the darkness, into what could be my own, and my battalion's deaths, everyone was quiet. In fact, surprisingly, the only person actually making a sound was Darlin McGinnis. Who kept muttering the rosary to himself, down and down the stairs, into the never-ending depths. As people pushed me and Charlie down, I had only my fear to face.

My son, my sweet son. Would I ever see him again? Would I die on a mission I barely understood? Of course not, I reassured myself. I would fight until I could finally have peace. Something was beginning to stir within me; I no longer was just in this war to keep my son alive. I also saw the injustices of the world in a new view. And I wanted to eradicate them.

We soon reached the bottom of the ship, and I looked around at the room which I had just entered. In doing so, my sense of fear only grew. The room I was in was on the -100th floor, according to a sign, placed next to the stairs which we had come down. Seeing what floor we were on did not calm me. The thought of millions of tons of pressure pushing down on me was not the only thing that sent chills down my spine though. What scared me the most was the only light, red and flashing, with the sound of a soft siren, constantly playing. I hated that sound; it was a sound which noted impending doom.

Thankfully, I wasn't alone, constantly people kept flowing down from the stairs behind me, and I was eventually forced out of everyone's way, and closer to the center of the room we had entered. I stressfully looked for Susan, and I was overcome with a sense of relief when I saw her stride down the stairs confidently. But it was not only infantry soldiers in the dark room I was in. Out of the shadows appeared a young man in a green military uniform who had dark skin, and gun slung across his shoulder. "Hello ladies and gentlemen!" The man shouted, "My name is Jerry, I will be instructing you all, and your squad leaders, on how we will be getting to the warzone!" As Jerry was saying this, he clapped his hands, and the dark room I was in got brighter when many large lights hanging from the ceiling turned on. Finally, showing how big the vast hall really was.

Upon turning on, these lights showed that the room probably went back for hundreds of yards. And all throughout the room, the lights illuminated large submarines (fractions of size of the Fransican), which hung off cranes from the ceiling, and below the submarines, were pools of water that sloshed back and forth with the movement of the ship. "These mighty vessels will take every battalion to their separate drop zones. I'm assuming all sergeants know the game plan," said Jerry. From all around me, I heard other men and women like me, sergeants, nod and agree with the man. But out of the corner of my eye I saw Charlie stare at me and try to mask a snicker. I was, however, still terrified, and did not find it amusing.

"Alright, I will be calling the sergeants forward. When you hear your battalion leader called, please follow them into the submarines. The submarines will be loaded with one battalion each, in order. Everyone ready. Good," spoke Jerry, not waiting for a response. "First up, Sergeant Frederic, go ahead,"

I then saw, who I assumed was Sergeant Frederic get up and walk to his sub with the rest of his crew. Each person stepped in bravely. They had no idea what this war was for, but they fought for it with unfaltering patriotism. As the last person of that battalion stepped into the submarine, the hatch into it closed. I heard a loud creaking sound, and with that I watched as the crane dropped the sub into black water.

The process of loading and dropping the submarines went on like this for a while. With all the sergeants being shipped to battle one by one. Person after person risking their lives for the country they loved. After more than half the submarines were loaded, and off to battle, Jerry called out into the vast chamber, "Sergeant Watson, please enter your sub."

I looked around for support from Charlie, but all he did was use his hands to shoo me forward. Taking a deep breath, I then trudged toward the next submarine up, which was on the far right. Reaching it, I looked back, to take what could be my last look at men who did not want to kill.

Turning forward, I walked into the submarine, which was fairly bland. It was illuminated by a few fluorescent lights and had chairs lining the sides of the back of it, but besides that nothing much. At the back it was slanted, and flat, and I assumed that was the part which would fall down so we could exit onto a raging storm of violence. Peering towards the bow, I saw the control room. It was occupied by two seats, each with a steering wheel, only one of which was filled. The man occupying it was unmoving and seemed incredibly dirty. Upon the control panel, I noticed many flashing buttons and levers, all of them sticky looking, and covered with grime. Looking at the number of them, I had to wonder what they were all for. Something else unusual about the submarine was the fact that there seemed to be no form of defense on it, there were no torpedoes, turrets, or anything. No weapons at all, which was confusing because we were going to war, and what is a war without weapons? *What was a world without weapons?* Another thing our government had taught us.

I sat down in a seat towards where I first had walked in so that I could see my battalion, specifically Susan, step into the submarine.

One by one, I greeted the men and women who I was leading. Starting with my good friend Charlie and ending with Susan. Susan sat down on the left side of me, and Charlie sat on the right side of me. Both people who I had connected with. Both of whom I had known a long time ago. All of us were part of a plot larger than we could imagine. The only people I had connected with in a long time. "Hi Susan," I said.

"How's your day going *Sergeant*," joked Susan.

"Who's this?" asked Charlie.

"Charlie, this is Susan, we were… college friends," I said, introducing both of my friends to each other. Charlie looked at me, smiling. "Susan Winter?" He asked. I nodded. "You had a thing for her before Kate!"

Embarrassed, I awaited Susan's response.

Susan laughed too, a beautiful laugh. "Well, nice to meet you."

I let the two of them shake hands and then waited for a little bit before a thought came to my head. "Hey," I said, "do any of you find it strange that we all come from college?"

"Coincidence?" Susan asked.

I shook my head. "And earlier General Myer asked me if I had known Charlotte Hive, who had also gone to Stanford the same year," I said.

Susan looked at me with a look of surprise on her face. "I had known her in college too."

"Me as well!" Charlie exclaimed. "She's the head of the Tahoen intelligence agency, right?"

"Yea," I replied.

Charlie put his hand on his chin pondering, "I'm sorry I ignored you earlier…"

We were all quiet for a while until Susan asked, "Who's the guy up front?" Pointing towards the sleeping man.

"Don't know," I replied, finding it hard to speak with the terror building up inside of me. It helped to be speaking to friends, but the threat of battle so very close was too much.

"Think he's dead?" Charlie said laughing, though I did not think it was funny.

"I am not dead. And you kids should know, it is very rude to talk about someone behind their back!" said the mysterious man, turning around in his chair to face me, Susan, and Charlie, startling us all. Luckily though, the man did not seem upset, in fact, he started to chuckle. "No hard feelings though, name's Derrick, Derrick Goodman, nice to meet you, and you are?" asked Derrick.

Shocked for a moment by the man's sudden vitality, I replied, "Oh, I... I'm Brian, and this is ... Charlie and Susan."

"Ah, and I'm guessing you're the sergeant of this crew, Mr. Brian!" Exclaimed Derrick taking a sip of beer which I had failed to notice on the control panel. It was smuggled in most likely. I nodded. "Anyways, I am going to get some more sleep before we go."

Derrick proceeded to put a dirty sailor's hat over his eyes and let his hairy arms fall to the ground. I started taking a closer look at the rugged man. He seemed around my age, maybe a little older, and was wearing a white polo, of which his large stomach stuck out of. He also wore jeans, though like the rest of him, they were dirty. He had a large nose, a brown beard, and many, many freckles. And though his appearance was horrendous, he had that feeling that radiated off of Charlie and Susan. An aura which was much different than your average person. Me and Susan both looked at each other and smiled.

While the man who I assumed to be the captain of the *mighty ship* slept (he didn't give us much information), I looked out one of the few tiny portholes. I watched as other people loaded into their subs and were eventually dropped to either their doom or a new life. Whether their fate was already laid out before them, or if it was up to them that they find a way to survive, it didn't matter. Either way, some would live on, and some would fall. With the drop of the submarine, they were locked into their fate, there was no longer any escape.

Some time passed, and I started to wonder why we hadn't gone yet. "Um, excuse me, Mr. Goodman. Shouldn't we have gone by now?" I asked timidly.

"Huh, mm, what," started Derrick, getting up with a jolt, and knocking over his beer onto the floor, which was thankfully already empty. Not paying attention to me or anyone else, in the noisy, full submarine, Derrick looked out the window at the front of the ship. "Good God, we should have already left! Only three submarines haven't gone. And they're part of the fifth attack! We were supposed to be in the second! Oh, Captain Herbert is going to have my ass for this! Why haven't they given me the signal on my walkie-talkie?" Derick asked himself, checking his belt where nothing hung. "Gone! Why is it gone!" For so many people in one area, I was surprised that Derrick had spent so much time talking to himself. So many lonely, in social society so full of people.

Opening the hatch to the submarine, none other than Captain Herbert himself stepped inside the vessel with impeccable timing. "Derrick!" He screamed. "Why haven't you taken these good soldiers to battle! You know General

Myer isn't going to like this, and neither is the president for that matter!"

"S--sorry sir. It's just you see my walkie–" stammered Derrick, trembling in fear.

"I don't care Derrick! Now go before I get you off the payroll!" Screamed the captain.

"Y-y-yes sir, right away sir," Derrick said, hitting a couple of buttons on the control board.

Captain Herbert grunted, obviously annoyed at the scruffy man. He turned to leave but quickly cracked a smile at me before he, saying, "Good luck sergeant," he nodded towards Susan and Charlie and then left quickly. But not before winking at me. No one else would realize what he meant by that, but I did. A hidden message behind the small gesture that seemed to fill me with hope, but also send daggers into my heart.

Me and Susan both then realized we were holding each other's hands, out of pure shock from the outburst we had witnessed. But we let go instantly before Charlie could laugh at me for too long. Still shaking from the captain, Derrick stood up from his seat, brushed off some crumbs from his shirt, took a deep breath, and quickly sat back in his chair, rapidly hitting buttons like on a keyboard. As he was doing this, I finally got up the courage to ask a question that had been bugging me out of alarm for myself. "Derrick, why aren't there any defenses on this submarine? Aren't we kind of exposed?" I asked curiously.

"You have nothing to worry about Sergeant Watson," Derrick said, not looking up. "We are completely safe."

I raised an eyebrow at this remark, for upon looking at the small vessel I was in, I realized how vulnerable we were. Once again safety had been put aside in order for men to become richer and profit off of everything. For this current time period it was the Cortezeon Plant being sold. In the future it will be something else. Most likely the weaponry of the vessel had been sold for scrap metal, or just not put on in order to cut costs. No matter how much we thought we had advanced as a species, we never moved forward.

An ancient philosopher had once talked of such a reality. In his time plastic was being used as the main material. However, a hundred years ago they had been using glass and tin, both of which could be recycled. Some of the plastics they used, however, were not recyclable however, but were used so the rich man could get richer. So, humanity had moved backwards in our evolutionary advancements even though time had gone by. I can't remember the philosopher's name, but we had not learned anything from what he had said.

Darlin looked back at me, and my thoughts dissolved. He said, "You might want to hold on to something though."

He quickly spun around to get a good view of the cabin and clapped his hands to get everyone's attention. "Everyone," Derrick said in a loud booming voice. "What you are about to do, could be the end of you, but that's ok. Because we are doing it for the greater good. And if you would all bow your heads, I'd like to say a prayer."

And as we went silent, able to hear each other's breathing, we became connected. I didn't listen to the words being spoken by Derrick, but they did something to us all. I watched as grown men cried, felt as I cried. We weren't sad, but we still cried. We became one, we felt each other's pain and knew that we had to do what we were doing to make a better future for our children.

I felt Susan's hand on mine but didn't move away. I just pulled it closer. And at that moment, I was proud to lead the people in front of me, I was ready to lead my first battle as a sergeant. At that moment it didn't matter what I was fighting for, it just mattered that I was fighting.

Nobody was really religious anymore, however no one cared. And I think one of the reasons we were all silent, and that we all prayed as one, was because we missed it. Missed the sense of unity we had left in the past. Forgotten, but not lost to the human soul.

In that moment Derrick must have done something then, because the next thing I knew, we were dropping down into the icy cold water, into its grip of death.

Chapter 9

As the submarine dropped down, down, down, into the pool beneath, I was reminded of my childhood. When I would go on rides almost like this and laugh myself silly. Though that thought brought me joy, it also brought me deep despair. What would Tim's childhood be like, if I died? Where would he go? Who would want to watch a child when it was already so hard to fend for oneself?

Upon hitting the water, my head jerked back, slapping against the hard plastic of my chair. Only another reminder of how little the military cared about its soldiers. To them we were just pieces on a chess board. I looked at Charlie, his eyes wide with fear, but a smile on his face as he held up a shaking thumb. The rest of my battalion seemed to be in a similar state.

We slowed in the water for a second, the submarine's headlights turning on to illuminate the dark water. We hung there in a still peace, and then Derrick pushed a lever forward. As he did this, I could feel the submarine lurch forward, and I almost lost my breakfast. Eventually settling down with the rest of the men, I took a chance to look outside of the ship. Try to take my mind off the moment and the thoughts of impending doom. What I saw was astonishing.

Lit up by countless lights, from submarines like the one I was in, was the H.M.S. Franciscan. So large, and wondrous, that I had to crane my neck to see the bow. Just yesterday I had seen the bodies of my fellow soldiers there (who I could be joining shortly if I wasn't careful). Beside it, strange, mutated organisms swam. Glowing with bioluminescence in the most beautiful shades of colors. No small animals were left, they had all died, killed by the bigger and stronger, those who were tougher. Still staring, Susan looked at my face, which was in awe. "Isn't it amazing what we can do? How small we are, and yet all the great and powerful things? Really makes you question it all. We are so small compared to this, imagine us compared to the rest of the world."

"You sound like Captain Herbert," I said, not looking back, my face still bathed in shimmering light.

"I do don't I." She laughed, "But he also said something else, something I think all of humanity should know."

"Oh?" I asked curiously.

"He said: 'What some people have been proving lately are two things, we are small, and we are monsters,'" Susan explained. "'And sometimes we are monsters because we want to prove we can be big.'"

For some reason, this statement prompted me to ask a question very quickly after. Something that I had not heard anyone ask. For everyone thought they knew the same answer. Everyone was told what to think. But I thought for moment about our size and what Susan had said, and I also thought of the rebels. A group of people who were going against what others thought. Going against the idea that we controlled all, that the A.R. was the best, that we were the most important when really, we weren't. They had killed Susan's family, so then why did I sympathize with them? I needed another opinion, and it felt like now might be a good time to ask, "Susan, what do you think about the rebellion?"

But just as she was about to reply, Charlie, who was next to us, was frightened by Derrick's sudden movement, and jumped slightly, disturbing Susan.

"Alright, quiet down, quiet down," Derrick said to the chattering crowd. "This vessel is on autopilot, so I thought I would take this time to say a couple of things. First of all, I'd like to apologize for the delay, though I'm sure, none of you were disappointed," saying that sent a ripple of chuckles down the stiff, terrified crowd.

179

"Anyway, I would like to explain some things. Many of you have asked me where your gear was. And I am happy to tell you, I have an answer!" Upon that, Derrick clicked a couple of buttons, and a creaking noise rang out throughout the submarine.

When the noise had subsided, racks of weaponry and military supplies came down from the ceiling of the vessel. They took up all available space that wasn't occupied, and I instantly started surveying what was around me, and noting what caught my eyes. "Feel free to take whatever you like. Medics, you'll find what you need in the back. Assault is on the starboard, and defense is on the port. We'll be making landfall soon though, so be quick." Derrick sat back down in his seat after saying all this and closed his eyes.

Before I could say anything to Susan or Charlie, they were both off and searching the containers for any gear they might need. On the other hand, I took time slowly profiling my options. It was hard with the number of people who crowded the lockers looking for anything that might help them survive, but I still managed to find some things I liked, and even got a chance to catch a glimpse of Susan from the other side of the ship.

Stepping up to one locker and then moving to another, the first thing I got my hands on was a bullet proof vest and helmet, hoping that the extra protection would give me a better chance to get home to Tim. It was large and heavy, but I sucked it up and put it on under my green uniform. The metal, like the Cortezeon Plant, was a modern wonder. Once again monopolized by the government. I then made my way to the other side of the boat and found an assault rifle, one of my favorite weapons of choice. Now, with the things I thought were the most important equipped, I then looked for extras that would only make things easier. A gravity grenade, a battle radio, and a tunneler. All "new" technologies according to the government, even though they had been invented in the 21st century. For some reason invention as a whole had seemed to stop.

When I made it back to my seat, Charlie and Susan were still gone, and Sam was the only person, besides Derrick, who was sitting down. But he was still polishing his machine gun, so I ignored him and focused my attention on Derrick, who was now awake and was wrestling with the controls of the ship. "Derrick, do you mind if I ask you a question?" I asked.

"Fire away kid!" Said the man, not looking up.

"Well, I was just wondering… who are we fighting in this war, I mean it's just one rock we're after, right?" I questioned.

"I don't think anyone knows kid. At one point every great nation is going to fall. The Romans, the Greeks, Australia, America. And I think this one," said Derrick waving his hand around, "is just about nuts and on the verge of falling. Though I do know one thing, we're just fighting whoever gets in our way. We could be fighting the Rohans, the Tahoens, even ourselves. All I know is that this country is planning on doing whatever it takes to get that stupid Dewa Ruci. All because they think it will save their own nation from economic collapse, stop *the fall*. Each country wants it for that reason. I think it's all stupid! They've gone mad with power!" Derrick then took a swig of his beer, grabbed the microphone once more, and screamed into it "Rising, rising, prepare for battle men! Remember if you can't take control of this island then the aircraft carrier can't get through!"

I looked down at my seat, trying to find a seatbelt. I quickly realized though that there was none. So, I just gripped onto my chair's handrails and closed my eyes. I looked around as the rest of my fellow soldiers ran back to their seats, though sadly in the confusion, I could not find

Charlie or Susan. Without the two of them, it was hard to get through a time like this. Keeping my eyes closed, I wrapped my hand around the locket that my wife, Kate, had given me the night she had died of ALS in that hospital bed. I had worn it ever since. Though that day, like the locket, was always with me.

It had happened on our anniversary. We had been married eight years, and Timmy was just two months old. We had been walking home from a lovely dinner, down the crowded, disgusting streets when it...

Kate started shaking, shivering almost, even though the weather was warm and tropical. I ran to her side. "Kate? Kate!" She didn't even seem to *see* me, she just looked up at the night sky, eyes darting left and right. Staring through me like I was a ghost. She sounded like she was trying to speak, but her words just came out as slurred nonsense.

The pain I felt as the ambulance arrived, taking her to the hospital… it was the worst I had ever felt in my life. That ride had been the longest of my life. Kate was technically awake, but seemed asleep, unmoving. Her heart stopped beating a few times on that ride, but they had kept her alive. When we arrived at the hospital, they ran tests and found she had ALS, which had gone undetected for the longest time. But it was already too late, there was nothing I could do. Still, I always think maybe we could have done something. If we had had more, if I could have given her a better life.

She had been placed in the hospital; she lived just days more before passing. I had stood there in the dark room, Timmy crying just because I cried. What could he have known, young as he was? I don't cry much, but when I do it's normally about something that really matters to me. I held her hand, and through the sounds of the city, and of the machinery, she spoke what I assumed were her last words. The doctors said that speech was impossible at her point. I could have sworn though that she murmured in my ears to take care of our son. Our one and only son who didn't even remember his mom. The one reason I was where I was now was because of him.

And though Timmy might not remember that day, I think about it always. Every person has a drive, the thing that keeps them going. My wife, my son, those were mine. And now, with Susan, I felt as if I was betraying her. I liked her, and I knew Kate would want this for me. Still though, it didn't feel right. Because in a way, if I had never met Kate, I might be with Susan and still have a wife.

Tears flowed from my eyes, though I tried my best to calm down. "Hey, you good?" I looked up to see Charlie sitting next to me, a confused look on his face. Susan was on the other side of the vessel, her face awash in concern.

"Yea, I'm fine," I replied, wiping away the tears.

"This battle is nothing to worry about, I mean, do you really think anyone else is going for Dewa Ruci?" Charlie asked.

"Yea, I guess not," I said, though after what Derrick had talked about, I now knew that to the rest of the world, this was no rock. This was salvation for some odd reason.

Up, up we went. Floating closer and closer to the surface, the light of the sun, glowing on my face. All until finally, popping to the surface, the submarine rocked back and forth. And then, we slowly cruised backward, almost like backing in a car. It was surprisingly quiet though, no sounds of war, no gunshots, no screaming, all I could hear was my heart beating, and my own breath. That was until, finicking with my walkie-talkie, I switched it to channel five. "Go, go, go!" Screamed a man on the other end.

"I need back up!" Screamed a woman.

"Medic," coughed another. The sound shocked the whole submarine. The gunfire, the screams, all horrendous. I had been in fierce battles, but I had not expected a battle for such a small island to be this hard. And this wasn't even for Dewa Ruci, this was for the island *next* to it!

Inching backwards we went. Slow and steady, until with a thud, we hit land. I looked towards Charlie once more for advice. But he only gave me a deathly grim look. I then looked toward Derrick, but he only sighed, made the sign of the cross, and pulled a lever above my head. And with that, a battle began in which I would lose many men, and my life would forever change.

Chapter 10

The first people to step out into the cloud filled, dirty sky got shot. Hit by the turrets, and the snipers hiding in the high and surprisingly green hills. A color I rarely ever saw, especially not naturally. A color and a view which was nearly identical to the spot of green on the hills except for the fact of scale. The cliffs were also full of birds, which flocked in to build nests high in the canopy. Even from afar I could see small creatures hopping from tree to tree. Life teemed. It was amazing, and hard to take my eyes from it. And somewhere I knew that in those hills were the rebels General Myer had spoken of. Maybe the only people that I could relate to. Even if some of them were killers. I could have stared at the greenery forever, basking in its beauty. But I knew, if I stood still, I would be slaughtered like the others before my eyes. That was one important thing war had taught me.

Charging out into battle, I pulled my assault rifle off my back, not looking behind myself, and jumped over the bodies of the fallen. With sand flying up from the ammunition coming from the cliffs, it was extremely hard to see. Left and right, explosions were happening, men were screaming. All in all, I was terrified. I knew if I wanted a fighting chance, I needed cover.

I scanned my harsh surroundings, still running, and eventually found a little ditch dug out from what looked to be a bomb explosion, a crater about the size of a small home. The leftovers of the enormous bomb which had created the difference in the terrain could be seen spread out all around. Pieces of shrapnel lay embedded in the sand and thrown out all about. I looked at the sky, trying to see what had dropped the weapon. But a dense fog was rolling in, and I couldn't see anything. The gorgeous blue of the sky, like the green of land, was a fading thing. However, I wondered why anyone wanted to bomb such a beautiful place. For even the beach was covered with small shrubs. Who were we fighting? What heartless people would destroy this?

I quickly jumped into the hole, sliding on the sand, my back toward the oncoming fire. And to my surprise I saw Charlie, blood dripping from his forehead, a gun in his hand, and his other hand on the trigger. He was leaned back against the sand, attempting to not get hit. "Hey sergeant!" Charlie screamed, smiling. "What do you want to do. Give the orders!"

"Right now," I wheezed, "I just want to go home!"

"Well, you figure that out, because we need a leader!" Charlie said, popping over the mound we were hiding behind, and firing a few shots.

Charlie was right though, all around me men were spread out, shooting aimlessly into the hills. With all this disorganized fighting, the Indonesians would just pick us

191

off one by one. Knowing I had to do something, I peered over my hiding place, looking for anything to target. Though all I saw were dead men, and way too many enemies. And all the hostiles were dispersed, so there was no good place to target. The Indonesians just hid in the hills, raining terror down on us all.

Wait!

That was it!

If they all hid in the hills, there would have to be a place for all of them to scurry around and get from place to place. Scanning the cliff side, I quickly found a small tunnel on the beach, that led straight into the mountain. "Hurry sergeant! We are losing men!" Charlie shouted, continuing to fire into the cliffs.

"Don't worry Charlie, I know what to do!" I said, immediately taking out my walkie-talkie. "All available men, please converge on point…" I stopped, looking down on my GPS watch, finding the coordinates of the enemy tunnel, "1.04471° S, 128.15603° E. located there is a small bunker which leads into the hills."

I peered at the location. A small concrete enclave buried into the mountain side. That was where we would go.

"Got it sergeant," I heard Sam say on the other line.

"Whatever you say," said Susan. I let out a sigh of relief knowing she was ok.

"Ok."

"Understood."

"Moving there now."

The responses flooded in, and with them I could feel myself being lifted up. Starting to realize how much faith my team had in me.

I turned to Charlie, "You ready?" I asked.

"Ready as I'll ever be!" He replied.

"Good," I said. "Find somewhere for us to take hunker down on the way!"

Charlie stared out across the vast expanse of beach. "There!" He shouted, pointing towards another of the many smoking craters in the ground, then ducking down just as a bullet whizzed dangerously close to his head.

"Alright, I'm running, you cover me!" I said, getting ready for a mad sprint. He nodded in return.

I took a deep breath, calming my heartbeat, and then jumped over my one form of protection from the oncoming fire, and into a barrage of bullets.

Immediately, every available gun turned on me, firing rapidly in my direction. The sand, shooting up, red hot, formed a cloud on me. But I kept running, pumping my arms and jumping over debris. One bullet even hit my armor directly in the chest, throwing me to the ground harshly. Though I quickly started moving again, bear-crawling towards safety. The crumpled shot falling to the ground in front of me.

Finally making it toward the edge of the hole, bruised and battered, I rolled into the pit. I looked back to see Charlie, still firing into the mountains. He saw me soon after though and stopped shooting. I waved him on. Now it was my turn to protect my friend.

Once more, I removed my weapon, rested it on my shoulder, took a deep breath, and… and stopped. The world seemed to freeze around me. The death, the screaming, the explosions of bullets, all gone. Just me and my thoughts. Which were telling me one clear thing. I couldn't do it. I had fought many battles in my life. I had sadly, shot and killed many soldiers. Though that had been for the freedom and life of the country which I had once loved. The country I was in now was different, it was dead. It was corrupt. Everyone, on this battlefield, I knew for a fact, did not want to be here. They did not support this war. We were fighting over one rock. One speck which we didn't even understand. And if we tried to ask questions… well, Captain Herbert said he would be killed for doing it. So, it was pointless, everyone was just too scared to admit it. I didn't want to fire back. Yet if I did not shoot at a scared, frightened enemy, who was just trying to defend their land, my friend would die.

So, I once more took a breath, peered over the crater I was in, aimed my gun at a poor man on the cliff who was clearly visible, and pulled the trigger.

With a thud the man fell to the ground, dead. I shed a tear, set my sight on a large turret, and started firing ravenously towards it. I had to help my friend.

Continuously shooting at the turret, bullets missing mostly, though some hitting it with sparks and a loud popping sound, I became the enemy's primary target. The man on the turret, looked at me, grinned, and spun the gun right towards me. Opening fire. Unlike the regular bullets though, these were big, and made small craters in the ground, along with their explosive sound that put a ringing in my ears. Of course, they were dwarfed compared to the crater I was in. At this point, I could no longer shoot my gun without getting myself shot, but I knew I had done my job. Charlie would be okay.

Putting my back against the sand wall, I watched Charlie dive into the new hiding place. Not a scratch on him. "Looks like you did a good job, Brian!" Charlie said laughing. "Now how are we supposed to get out of here?"

I frowned. By solving a problem, I had just condemned us to the same fate just in a different place. I felt as if I had failed. How could I, just another human in a sea of others, make a difference, how could I do something good?

There *had* to be something we could do; I had to get home. I looked around the hole I was in, trying to assess the situation, and trying to answer the question in my head. How could we make it home?

Thankfully though, my question was answered soon. I felt a twitching beneath my left leg, and looked down, only to discover the sand behind me was caving in. Charlie must have noticed too, because at the same time we backed up as much as we could, and both nearly jumped out of our skin from surprise, when none other than Lieutenant Sam Tyler popped his head out of the sand. "Oh. Hello Sergeant Watson. Charlie," said Sam, a tunneler in the large man's hand.

Seeing Sam, I was filled with hope. Sam had dug to our location. That meant we could dig to the enemy! I didn't have to think of an answer, Sam already had. My team had. And for the first time since my wife died, I realized that I wasn't alone.

Climbing out of the tunnel, came nearly half of my crew, all following the strong man. Even Darlin McGinnis came crawling out, surprisingly still alive. I guess everyone knew, nobody could get through Sam. I turned back towards Charlie, and now Susan was with me. They were among the rest of my crew, Charlie smiled, obviously thinking the same thing as me. "Everyone," I shouted, the pride to lead my crew into battle welling up inside of me, "if we don't do something, we will be picked off one by one like rodents. We need to dig! Follow me!"

I pulled the tunneler off my back, hitting the "on" button, which lied on the strange mechanism, and it began rotating rapidly. The tunneler had been invented in the late twenty-first century as a way to dig underneath buildings and cause them to collapse, (wasn't it strange how whole innovation had stopped once the Cortezeon Pill had been marketed?) and it wasn't the prettiest thing. It was what looked to be a kitchen whisker on steroids. But it had helped me before, and I was sure it could help me now. Even if it wasn't going to be doing what it was meant to do.

Pushing the tunneler into the soft sand, I started off by slowly pulling the trigger, which got the front of the machine turning even faster. Once the rest of my crew saw what I was doing, they too began our escape. Pushing down into the damp, golden sand proved no challenge. We quickly covered a great distance, over 20 people on their hands and knees, digging down. Burrowing underground to escape the horrors of the world above us. I knew we were getting closer though, when the sand turned to soil. "Almost there!" I shouted.

We picked up our pace, our nails sinking into the damp dirt. Soon, I was surprised to see what looked like string hanging from the ceiling. It was something I had never seen before. Yet strangely, I felt that deep down somewhere, buried in my DNA, I knew what they were.

"Hey, does anyone know what's on the ceiling?" I asked curiously.

At first, no one spoke up, so I assumed they were unimportant. But then, from behind me, I heard Darlin speak up. "Yea. They're well, they're roots. You know, from trees."

"Trees," I muttered in wonder.

"Yea, trees. Roots give them water," Darlin said. "Does anyone else know what I'm talking about?"

The rest of my crew muttered the same answer in unison. "No". Even though I had just gone to the zoo, seeing trees. The zoo, I knew, had modified the genes of trees and animals before that science was outlawed and destroyed. Messed with their genetics, they made them more cost-effective. It would make sense to take away roots because they went in the soil and there wasn't much of that. And if it was allowed, I bet that people would have just changed more of the beautiful creatures. Attempting to make a profit like General Myer, and most of the world. "How… how do you know Darlin? How d-d-do you know they're not just cobwebs?" asked Sam.

"I read about it. You know trees used to be an everyday thing you saw, same with roots. But now they're not."

Still digging through the earth, I couldn't help but look up at the roots that dangled from the roof, and long to see what they were attached to. I couldn't let myself get distracted though. There was a battle to be fought.

Continuing to stare up at that one part of a tree, my thoughts were interrupted by a loud bang and shaking that came from above. Dust fluttered down, sprinkling onto the floor. "Nobody move," I whispered.

Nothing happened, all was still and calm, and then, through the void of sound, I heard a loud rumbling sound which was unmistakably the sound of a plane. Louder and louder it became, closer and closer, until… just as quickly as it came, it was gone. Everyone looked up, staring at the ceiling, sitting still in complete silence, the only sound was the soft hum of the tunnelers.

And then there was another noise.

It wasn't loud, like the rumbling of the plane's engine, it was the whistling of something much more sinister. As the sound got nearer, I looked towards the rest of my crew, ready to scream, but their faces remained unchanged, just curious. And just as I was about to tell everyone to run, the bomb hit. And I knew what had made the craters in the sand.

Chapter 11

With a bang that left my ears ringing, part of the ceiling collapsed. "Everyone out!" I shouted. Though I didn't need to tell anyone. Already, I could hear the sound of more planes roaring and bombs falling, and I was sure the rest of my men did too. Left and right, holes opened in the roof, and with them chunks of the gorgeous roots and dirt fell away, threatening to crush anyone left behind. I wanted to find out who this third party was, who was attempting to destroy us, but I knew I would have to be outside for that. I would also have to be outside if I wished to survive.

Digging faster now, there was no looking back. Dirt was falling in my face, but I blinked through it, because I knew that if I stopped not only would I die, but so would my friends; the people relying on me. So, I kept digging. Digging, digging, digging. The roof continued to collapse, light beaming in from the sky above through the dust in the air.

With a loud bang above me, once again, a large bomb exploded. With the shaking of the earth, chunks of dirt and rock plummeted down, caving in the tunnel ahead of me, and thankfully not behind me where my crew lay. "We have to keep going!" I yelled behind me over the chaos, turning around to see a dirty Charlie, blood dripping from his face, a small smirk on his lips.

I turned to my left to avoid a boulder that blocked our path, and then started back on course, praying not to get lost. On and on we went, constantly running from the danger above. Finally, thinking we had gone far enough, I looked down at my GPS watch in the insanity we were in, to see if we had reached the coordinates I had marked. Sadly though, the watch was cracked, and shards of glass were stuck in my arm. The tons of rock above me shuddered once more, sending a shiver down my spine. I took a deep breath and looked above me. We better be here. Angling the tunneler towards the surface, I breathed in the dusty air, and hoped we did not just surface only to be shot.

Digging against the hard earth, I could feel my heart beating out of my chest, felt my friend's hot breath against my neck, and heard gun fire from outside. Hopefully this wasn't the end, it couldn't be. Then, the earth gave way, and I felt the sensation of the cold outside breeze hit the musky air of the tunnel beneath me.

I pulled the device back in and turned around to look at Charlie. "Wait here," I said quietly, the bombs having seized as quickly as they had arrived.

He nodded.

Sticking my head out just enough so that my eyes could see, I made a 360 degree turn to find out where we were. I started by noting thankfully that the beach was far away, the white caps breaking onto metal spikes which lined the shore which was painted with blood. Now to find out if we had made it to the bunker that was buried in the hills. Turning the opposite way, I was thrilled to see we were right next to the mountain, and even better, I saw we were next to something manmade set into the cliff. It had to be the bunker. I was just about to shout with joy when I nearly had a heart attack. There, standing on watch, was a tall, muscular man with a gun in his hand. He was peering out of the cavern, looking out towards the sea, thick sunglasses covering his eyes.

I slowly went back into the tunnel where my crew still waited. I held up my finger to my lip. Charlie nodded in response, and then he too slowly came up to survey our enemy. Retreating in, Charlie looked at me for our next move. "What should we do sergeant?"

"Well, we could try to knock him out, but I don't know how. And we would have to make it unnoticeable; we don't want anyone finding out where we are," I said trying to figure out our next step while battle still raged behind us.

At that moment, the whole tunnel started arguing, our voices getting louder and louder. The arguing went on and on, some people wanting to kill the man, some wanting to spare him, and others just wanting to give up. The only person not talking was Sam, who just sat there staring off into space. Luckily though, after some time passed, he made the decision for us. With the roll of his eyes, Sam took out a pineapple grenade, popped the pin, and threw it up into the bunker. With a loud boom, it went off. We all stared at him. "What are you all waiting for, I just set off an explosion, people will be coming!" We all just stared at him. "Just go!" Screamed Sam.

Instantly we all scurried out of the tight chamber. I looked over the wall that led into the gloomy room. A miraculously large tunnel, it just went right into the dimly lit mountain, which then split into separate tunnels. It was like a maze. Helping the rest of my crew out of the hole-in-the-ground proved no physical challenge, though my heart was beating very fast. I knew why. I was petrified. Not only could my crew die, but I might have to murder more people, and I did not want to have to harm anyone else. I was done being a soldier, I wanted to help others, not help a corrupt government.

I had a feeling that after this mission was over (if I made it out), I would retire. No longer did I care if I didn't have the money, I just wanted to get back to Tim, maybe even live at the rest of my days on that green hilltop... Right now, that was my *real* mission.

"Hey," said Darlin, looking out of the cavern and into the beach, "those planes. Those are Tahoen planes!"

I turned my head to the sky, and there, dropping bombs, were Class 5 Hover-Bombers. The Tahoen Navy's top military jet. Nuclear powered, and capable of reaching the speed of sound and flying in place, they were very dangerous. The murmurs that went through the men were static, all about how we had been betrayed by our allies, how it wasn't right.

After the A.R. stabbed the former British during WWIII in the back, soon after their government was reformed. And after that we quickly allied with them.

Just as these whispers of hate, and fear were being spread, one of the bombers turned towards us. Coming in at a steep angle. Everyone started backing up, some turning into a mad sprint to avoid the incoming terror, others just cowering in the sand. Then it opened fire, raining terror down upon us all. I jumped into the sand, covering my head. Right over our heads it sailed, pulling up at the last second to avoid crashing into the green mountain side. Some men were hit, flying to the ground. Bright red blood splattered on the sand.

I exhaled; thankful it didn't bomb us. The outcome would have been much worse. "We should probably get inside!" I spat into the muttering crowd. "Grab any wounded… leave the dead."

My battalion got to work, pulling any injured soldiers into the darkness, tending to what wounds they could, taking the dog tags of those who they could not. My men, dead. My battalion a fraction of what it had originally been. Somehow my friends had made it through, but how much longer could I protect them? As I watched the terrible scenes play out in front of me, Sam turned to me. "Sir, allow me to go first."

"Oh," I said, "shouldn't I go first, I mean I'm the sergeant and all."

"True sir, but um. My gun is bigger," Sam said, holding up his massive machine gun.

"Then please, after you…" I replied, sticking out my hand to gesture the large man in.

As Sam stepped into the dark chamber, and I followed, I instantly felt something was off. We were stepping into enemy territory, and Sam was acting... weird. I gripped the cold metal of my gun firmly, ready to pull the trigger. I looked down for a second but regretted it instantly. The guard's body was spread out all over the place. Keeping my eyes forward on the creeping shadows, I crept forward until I was shoulder to shoulder with Sam, my fear rising. "Flashlights on," Sam said, not looking back.

Again, Sam was acting strangely, taking my power.

Moving ever so slowly forward, yet going farther and farther into the gloom, I realized something I should have thought of sooner. "Wait, where are we going?"

"Communications tower, there's one on the third floor," Sam whispered.

"How do you know where that is, I didn't see anything from outside?" asked Susan, who was beside me now. Thankfully unharmed by the series of events.

"I… studied the schematics," Sam said. "They had some on the Bima."

"Why weren't we notified?" Asked a man from the back rudely.

"Doesn't matter, now keep quiet."

I looked through the dark at the muscular man. Something was fishy, yet I didn't know what. "Up the stairs, everyone," Sam said, nodding towards a twisting flight of stairs that lead up the mountain.

Though I was starting to distrust the man, I had no choice but to follow Sam. So up we went. Further towards the peak of the mountain. Until questionably, we stopped on the second floor. "Sam… we're n-not on the third

floor?" Darlin said skittishly.

We had stopped in front of a propped open door

which led into a hallway. It overlooked the horrific

battlefield. It was filled with large turrets which had

previously been shotting at us, however at the moment it

looked deserted. "This hallway will get us close to the

communications tower, after that we only have another

flight of stairs." Sam replied.

Stepping into the room, it seemed to be empty

besides some weaponry and crates on the ground. I couldn't

shake the feeling though that this wasn't a good idea. The

room seemed to be very strategic, and silly to leave

unoccupied. We carefully walked through the building;

outside was chaos. All seemed calm where we were

though, perfect peace as we lurked down the corridor. Far

off in the distance I could still hear the screams of the

dying, the men who I had lost. The place itself though

looked like... home. Like something the A.R. would have in the Juan Cortezeon Institute. So then why were they the enemy?

Soon, we heard footsteps coming. Echoing off the walls. I looked towards Sam in horror. He looked back and quickly hid behind a pile of boxes full of ammunition. The footsteps got closer. And then they were right in front of me. It was one man, thin and scared. He seemed just as shocked to see me and my battalion as I was him. He raised his rifle. Shouting at me in a language I didn't understand, though I could tell he was terrified. I dared a glance at Sam who was now behind the man. He put his fingers to his lips. The man continued shouting, and I put my hands in the air. The rest of my crew did not have their weapons out; some were in fact still holding their tunnelers. He stuck the gun in my face and pointed at the rest of my battalion.

Then, ever so slowly, Sam got to his feet, crept behind the soldier, and pulled out a 9-inch knife. The man continued shouting. Sam then, as gently as possible, slid the knife in one clean, firm motion over the man's throat. Blood hit the cool pavement and the man's body fell. Right before it hit the ground Sam caught it. Setting it down without a sound. We continued moving like it was nothing. Like we had not just killed a man.

I was starting to trust Sam more now that he had saved us, my worries were fading. We made it to the second staircase, all the while looking out onto the beaches where explosions were going off and the cries of men filled the air. We climbed the stairs quietly. On and on we went. And at one point we passed the third floor.

"Sam that was the third–" I spoke.

"Change of plans, that one's compromised. We will go to the other communications tower," Sam said.

"There's another communications tower?" I asked.

"Everyone keep moving, we have no time," Sam said, fully ignoring my question.

That was it. I was the leader, and it was time I acted like one. I was sick of being treated like I didn't matter, and it was my fault men had died, and I had to take responsibility. "Sam, stop," I said, standing still.

"Just keep moving," Sam said, already halfway up the next set of stairs.

"Stop."

"Keep moving."

"Stop."

"Onward."

"Sam, stop!" I yelled.

That was a mistake. My shout echoed throughout the series of hallways, and rooms that twisted through the mountain. Alerting every living thing to our position. Sam glared at me, and everyone else just looked around, listening for any movement.

Footsteps. Loud, thundering footsteps. A sound most people should be acquainted with, and yet now, it was terrifying. My fear welled up inside of me, like a balloon ready to pop.

"Run!" I shouted. There was no need to be quiet now, the whole mountain knew our location.

I grabbed a door on my left and flung it open, only to find armed guards a hundred yards away from me and running fast in my direction. Grabbing Susan who was about to step out with me, we raced up the stairs. My whole crew was with me. Gunshots rang out in our direction. There was no time to worry about why Sam wanted to keep going up.

Running up the steps, I didn't dare look behind me in fear that it would slow me down. Sam though, eventually passed me, which only prompted me to question him even more. In fact, Sam ran so fast that I could not even see him, for he had gone behind the bend of the next set of stairs in front of me.

Panting, heaving, my chest felt like it was about to burst, but I continued to climb. Never looking back and never stopping. That was until I saw Sam standing at the top of one of the stair sets, breathing heavily. "We can't go any farther," he gasped. "We've reached the top."

My heart sank at his words. "Is there a room at the top?" I asked, a plan formulating in my mind.

"Yes," responded Sam, "why?"

"Get everyone to that room, I'll make sure no one gets left behind," I said, running back down the stairs.

"But…" shouted Sam down the stairs, however I was already sprinting away.

Bounding down the stairs, back to my team who was coming up, I went so fast, I skipped steps, just leaping from one set, to the next, my feet feeling the impact like a car hitting a wall. Finally, when I was close enough to the oncoming enemies that I could see them firing bullets into the crowd of people rushing up the stairs, I stopped. I had come down quite a lot, and now I could see our enemies were only a few yards below myself, coming at me quickly. They chased my team up, shooting down one after another. Comrades falling.

Panting hard, I had no time to catch my breath. Armored soldiers, dressed in black, with helmets and bullet proof vests on had already spotted me. Bullets flying over my head and shooting sparks off the concrete wall behind me, I was forced to crouch down behind my only cover, a short metal hand railing. As the shots rained down on me, men and women who I was supposed to protect came crawling forward, bloody and bruised, dodging bullets which grazed their heads, though some of them were not so lucky. Going lifeless and dead, just feet from my face. This reminded me of what Susan had explained, she had said all humans are monsters. Though I had to push through those thoughts, my crew needed me.

Pulling anyone I could forward, trying to save them from a fate others had suffered, I shouted the same thing to each of them. "Get to the top, don't stop, don't look back, don't worry about me!"

Person after person went, no one questioned me, all running from the ever-advancing enemy. All except one. Over the loud screams and gunfire of the warzone, one man stopped, the last of my surviving battalion who had not gone to the top floor. Pulling him down beside me just as someone shot at him, I said what I had said to all of my men, "Get to the top, don't stop, don't look back, don't worry about me!"

"Are you crazy, I'm not leaving you sergeant," said the man.

I stared at the man, bruised and battered; he would not leave me. And staring at him, I realized who it was, it was Darlin McGinnis. Timid, shy, Darlin McGinnis! But it couldn't be, and yet it was. I could see the same fear that was there earlier in the day, but he was different. He wanted to help. Looking at the man who that same day had been scared to talk to me, and now who was willing to give his life for me, I realized where Susan had been wrong. Yes, some humans could be monsters. But others could be heroes.

Still crouching with me, Darlin looked over his shoulder, noticing the soldiers that were just starting to turn a corner and notice us. "Time to go Sergeant Watson." Heaving me off the ground, Darlin took out a handgun and fired two rounds at a soldier who was starting to raise his gun, and with loud bang, the man dropped dead. "I thought you were a technician's officer?" I asked, not thinking the man even knew how to use a gun.

Darlin shrugged, starting to run up the stairs, "Desperate times call for desperate measures. And besides, Sam told me that you could use all the help you could get."

"Yea about Sam," I started, quickly turning around to shoot another person coming up the stairs. "he's been acting awfully suspicious."

"Yea, he did tell me to turn off my radio for no reason, I just assumed he wanted it to be quiet though," Darlin replied.

Still climbing the many stairs, and still struggling for air in the hot, sticky climate, Darlin turned to face me and must have seen the concern in my eyes. "And that's most likely the case. I trust Sam. And what, you think Sam didn't want us to be warned that this was all a trap or something?" Darlin finished just as we reached the top floor and stepped into the room that was there.

"Yes, it is a trap!" Shouted Sam, standing tall and proud in the door frame.

Chapter 12

What was happening sent more terror into me then getting killed. Which at the moment was a very real possibility.

"Zack, Sandy, please put these two with the rest," Sam spoke.

With that note, two large, strong men came over and cuffed me and Darlin with sterolined cuffs. The handcuffs paralyzed the hand of the wearer, making escape nearly impossible. Once again, an incredible invention being used for evil. Once I was secure, my captor then dropped me at the front of the room where a large lookout was, staring out over the battlefield. The man with Darlin took him to a group of my soldiers, all of whom looked disappointed in themselves. I caught Susan's eyes. They were filled with tears.

As I sat there, looking out into the gory horror below on the beach, I began to choke up. Bombs fell from the sky; artillery hit the sand in smoking bursts. Offshore a massive aircraft carrier floated, and bombers ran runs on it. I took a glance to survey my surroundings. I had been in a prisoner of war before, and if there was one thing I knew, it was that you had to know your prison and your captors. The room itself was built for war, though the Indonesians, or whoever the enemy was, had added their own touch to the place.

All around, large computers and weaponry tables stood, men in military gear surrounding each one. Holograms and advanced technology placed in a place that looked oddly primitive. It had the same sterile feel as the Franciscan, not the dirty feel of the rest of the world. Whoever Sam was working with, they had to be a world superpower. Still exploring the room, I overheard a couple of guards muttering to each other, though surprisingly, they were not speaking in a foreign language, they were speaking in English, with just the hint of a British accent in their voices. The same accent people in the nation of Tahoe used. "So, it's true!" I shouted at Sam, a lump in my throat. "These aren't just the Indonesians, these are Tahoens!"

I got a response but not from the person who I expected to hear from. A figure hidden in the shadows, a woman, snapped at me in her own strong accent. "Feels bad to be betrayed, doesn't it you *Andy*. Well, I was betrayed by your country and now everyone I love is dead. Killed because they had known too much and had seen what your country was doing wrong. You've been tricked now, not just by us, but by our own nation. And don't act like you don't know the truth, you know that your country hasn't told you the full story, Sergeant Watson!"

Squinting my eyes to see in the gloom, out stepped a tall, slim woman, with short black hair that was cut at the neck, and was covered with a grey military cap. It was the

227

same color as her skirt and long coat. She was the head of Tahoen Intelligence and was known around the world as Charolette Hive. "Hello Miss. Hive," I said through gritted teeth.

"Good to see you still remember me Brian, after all, college was a long time ago. I can remember it like it was yesterday, you and Kate. Not anymore though," said Charolette.

"I'll kill you!" I screamed, trying with all my might to move my hand which the cuffs held. And then it hit me. I knew why I was leading my battalion, and I knew why I had been given this position. The raise, the promotion, the lies… All of it so that they could use me in their own plans. "They sent me out to find you," I muttered.

"Yes, and Charlie and Susan, a team they thought would allow you to know what my next move was. But we had our own plans." Charolette saw my dismay, and clucked her lips before saying, "Poor Sergeant Watson don't take this personally. You didn't have to lose her either, you know. We could have lived a happy life together, Brian. However, that will never be. You will die now, like her, but not yet. Now I want you to watch your country die. After all, the only reason you're here is because Sam told me your battalion had the chance to stop me. So, I had to take action. Still, not your fault.

For the only reason I'm here is to avenge my family. Your country is the only reason they're dead, and that is the only reason I'm taking part in any of this." finished Charolette.

"What's on Dewa Ruci?" I suddenly asked.

However, Charolette just turned to me and smiled, saying, "Asking questions like that is the reason my family is dead." She strutted up to the window where she could see that battlefield and stood with her hands behind her back.

"Prepare to see your Kate, Brian." She looked at a man behind a large screen and computer and spoke, "Cripple their carrier and destroy the island. Only people in this bunker will survive."

"What about our men fighting on the beaches?" One of her own men asked.

Charolette frowned and then stood there for a moment. "We need to make sure no one but us can get to Dewa Ruci." She spoke. "We have other soldiers... but this is the A.R.'s full force.

"You see, only now have we been able to bomb your military, Brian. Because for years you've been hiding behind your anti-air systems, but now, with your army away from any defense..." The two men flipped a couple of switches and inserted two shining keys into slots. When they twisted them simultaneously, an alarm began to sound.

Sam's eyes widened. "My family is on the island, Charolette, you can't do this. This wasn't the deal, you promised me my family would be safe, you promised me! You know better than anyone what I've been through!" screamed Sam, Zack and Sandy coming up to restrain the large man as he attempted to run towards Hive.

"Which is why I must do this, Sam. This may be our only chance to destroy the A.R.'s army, and I must. So that they don't hurt more people like my family," replied Charolette, wiping a tear from her eye.

"His family's on this island?" I asked.

"I said he was mercenary, didn't I? His family is being held hostage, they have no protection and will die with the rest of the A.R." said Charolette.

"Monster," Charlie said from the back of the room, lying on his knees.

Hearing him, Charolette turned her body in a creepy, robotic way and walked towards my friend. "I'd be quiet if I were you, because you have exactly ten minutes before your country is blown to ashes and there is no way you can stop this because if you have failed to notice, you are chained up. The only reason you are even still here is because the great nation of Tahoe has realized that you only follow the A.R. blindly and have no idea of their true malice. You will be held prisoner as we try to convince you what your country has done wrong… all of you except Brian. He will be a good example for you all."

"We're the villains?" Charlie asked.

"Though you are taught that your nation is almighty, the greatest, the most merciful, in truth you are all the most despicable speck of dust this universe has ever seen."

Speck. I felt that I had heard that word before, or at least others like it. A word that sent anger into my bones, a word that made me feel stupid, a word that made me feel small. Sam must have been thinking the same thing as me, because in the time after Charolette's speech to Charlie, under his breath Sam whispered, "Are you saying my family is worthless?"

"Pardon?" Charolette asked.

"Are-you-saying-my family-is-worthless!" Screamed Sam, still being held back by men that were half his size.

"We're almost all small and insignificant in this world Mr. Tyler," said Charolette, the sirens still blaring. "It is only the smart that can see that though."

Sam screamed out in rage, knocking back the two men holding him down. With bullets flying past his head, I watched from my position on the ground as the large man leapt across desks and computers towards the controls which would shut off the attack. Bullets flying past his head, I could tell the man was ready to die for his family, die for a good cause. Reaching for the desk, Sam dove about four feet, and just before he was about to pull out one of the keys which would stop the barrage of missiles, a shot louder than the rest rang out. Sam lurched in an awkward way, hitting the ground with a thud, and landing so that his back was laid up against the controls. A gaping wound in his shoulder. "Sorry Sam, you knew the stakes," Charolette said, panting and holding the shotgun which had fired the shot which had pierced Sam's arm.

"Yes, I did," Sam said with a heaving breath.

Throwing his hand back, Sam twisted one of the keys out of place, and with it the alarm went off. Though another sound took its place, with a second loud bang, Charolette Hive shot Sam once again, killing him. "Nice doing business with you," said Charolette. Though in her voice there was touch of sadness, as if she didn't want to kill someone who had a family. "I'm sorry, but it is time I finally avenge those I love. The A.R. will not kill another innocent. You were just in my way. Prepare the strike again, time is not something we have a lot of."

I was astonished by Sam's performance even though he had failed. He had easily known he would be killed, and that his actions would be fruitless, but he had done what he had done out of pure love. And since this astonished me, I thought that maybe we actually *were* the villains.

Charolette was walking away and giving orders, telling others to start the attack again, when from Sam's bloody, limp hand rolled out a pineapple grenade with no pin. The grenade rolled out until it was mere feat from Charlotte. "Huh, what's this?" The woman asked, staring down at the grenade. Charolette Hive's eyes widened, and just as she was about to scream, Miss Hive learned that

revenge did not always come easy.

Chapter 13

I awoke in a hospital bed, wet and cold. I sat up with a jolt, nearly hitting General Myer who was standing above me, watching me intently. "Whoa easy there Mr. Watson, you've been through quite a lot of trouble."

I tried my best to calm my breathing, which was heavy because of the moist jungle air.

Jungle! I turned around to see if my senses lied to me. I was in a makeshift canopy, drooping with water from the hot, sticky rain that came from outside. Doctors and nurses rushed in and out of the pop-up hospital, trying their best not to trip on the sand from the beach. All around me there were hospital beds, just like mine, full of injured people. Their moans filled the air with an eerie sound. I looked up at the general who stared at me puzzled.

"Oh, I'm sorry." I spoke. "I thought I might... that I might see trees."

General Myer laughed. "There'll be plenty of time for that, but from what Mr. McGinnis tells me, you need to rest!"

"Wait, how... how'd I get here?" I asked.

"You were knocked out from falling debris, you're lucky Sam's grenade didn't kill you... others were not so lucky," General Myer said solemnly, but quickly putting a smile on his face. "After that, thanks to your team, we were able to capture the beach. We are currently clearing out the rest of the enemy."

"Who didn't make it?!" I asked, concerned for my friends' safety.

"Don't worry, that monster Sam has paid for his crimes, his actions nearly destroyed the A.R..." I rolled my eyes at the man; I had forgotten how much he cared for his country. A country which, according to Charolette, was evil.

"Who!" I pulled off the hospital blanket, putting my wobbling, scraped feat on the ground. "Who didn't make it!" I screamed

Myer took a deep breath, "Before I tell you, I'd like you to know that the loss of your battalion was not your fault, it was Sam's," finished General Myer, pounding his fist into his hand.

"First, with all respect sir, it is my fault, I should have stopped Sam. He was looking suspicious. He was a part of my battalion and was my responsibility. And second, Sam was being blackmailed, he was a good man just trying to protect his family... I would have done the same, any good father would," I put my head down, attempting to calm myself. The general was dumbfounded. "Now, General Myer, would you please tell me who was killed in there."

"Charlie!" Darlin screamed, limping forward before the stubborn man could speak, Susan by his side. "Brian, I'm sorry, Charlie didn't make it out… and Charolette got away. One of her *goons* jumped down on the grenade to protect her. Sacrificed their own life."

"What are you doing here Mr. McGinnis? I thought you were supposed to be with the others, flushing out locals. Or doing something on a computer or whatever," said General Myer through clenched teeth.

"Today I don't feel like killing people general, instead, I feel like helping people. For the rest of the day, I will be in the infirmary, tending to the wounded," replied Darlin.

"So, will I," said Susan, rushing to me. "I was so worried about you! When that explosion went off… all hell broke loose," she gave me a big hug which hurt my side. I probably had a broken rib.

I blushed, "I'm ok," I said. At the time I was trying to hold back tears. I had lost another.

"Yes, well Mr. Watson needs no help thank you very much," with that note from General Myer, Darlin walked away with a scoff. Susan stayed. "Anyways, I wasn't planning on telling you about the news until later, though you seem to have taken it fairly well. Isn't that right Sergeant Watson? Watson? Mr. Watson?"

From that point on I stopped listening, I could tell that my general and Susan were both still talking, but it was as if I had left my body. I was too lost in thought. My best friend, my only friend had just died. I'm not saying Darlin wasn't my friend, and Susan was really special to me, and I had fun with them, but that's the point. Charlie connected with me; he sympathized with me. Sure, he was big and clumsy. But he was good, and that was not something you found in people often. I didn't want to believe it, and yet I knew it was true that Charlie was my *only friend*. But it was true. I didn't want to believe he was dead. But it was true.

Though the Juan Cortezeon Military Institute was full of people, I rarely noticed my fellow soldiers. We ate together, worked together, we lived together, and yet no one really got to know each other. Only when I had reconnected with old friends had I finally felt as if I was loved. Though that had ended.

People were supposed to live forever; it was the way of life. Our lives were huge and important; we could do great things. Except that we could never, truly, live forever. I now realized something, Charolette was right about one thing, we are all specks. Nothing but a grain of sand in the scale of the universe. Even someone as large as Charlie was small.

But would Charlie think that? No. Charlie was a soldier, and he knew what was right. Though it is good to remember how small we are, we must also remember those few amazing things we can do. Without Charlie's help, I couldn't have made it to the control room, Charlie covered me while I ran across a battlefield. In turn bringing Sam with us and stopping the destruction of thousands... even if he had never made it back alive. One small person did something great with their sacrifice. I would do the same. A wise person once told me humans are two things, we are small, and we are monsters. I recognized I was small, and I also recognized there were monsters all around me.

I snapped back to a scared general and Susan, who both were looking at me with concern. "Sir, I am feeling much better," I lied, shocking General Myer with my sudden movement, "You said something about flushing out locals, I'd like to help."

…

As I walked out of the tent that protected me from the rain outside, Susan caught up with me. "Brian what are you doing!" she yelled at me as the rain hit her face, soaking her hair.

"I'm done standing on the side lines! I'm doing something!"

"By... killing people?" She asked confused.

"I'm not going to kill them, I'm going to save them. And after that I'm going to stop Charolette. We were all put in this battalion to stop her, and I'm going to do that, not for Myer but for Charlie. She didn't want to kill us, but anyone who is going for Dewa Ruci is cruel, not just the A.R...I can feel it."

She smiled. "You're a good guy Brian Watson. Even if you're going to betray your country."

"This country died years ago." I stared off into the green hills. The trees were speckled orange with flowers that would occasionally blow off in the wind. One such flower floated down and landed in Susan's hair. I picked it out. Such untainted beauty, why had we ever gotten rid of it? I put my nose to the flower; it smelled incredibly sweet. I yearned more than ever to just be home.

Susan came over and gave me a peck on the cheek. I realized then this was what my wife would want.

Both Susan and I walked off to different places, both of us going to save people, just in different ways. I knew my decision was a good one. Killing a blameless people was not something I would do, and thankfully my general had bought it that I liked harming the innocent. I smirked, the man had just thanked me for my service and given me a pat on the back. He barely cared that I could die. He had one goal, and he was willing to do anything to get there. And at that moment, a spark inside of me began to grow into a blazing inferno. I had my mission, and I, like General Myer, would do anything to get it.

Rounding the corner that led me behind the tent, where I knew I would find the massacre of locals, my mouth dropped. I had read books, seen pictures and videos of them, had gone to the zoo even, but what I saw brought tears to my eyes. I saw green, so much green. When I breathed the air felt refreshing and cool, unlike the thick and almost poisonous air of home. Looking up into the trees, they reminded me of the buildings and skyscrapers which I was so familiar with. And I could see why we built our homes so similar to them, we missed them. Missed the lives we used to know when we lived among giants, when birds and small creatures were all around us. We had killed something we loved so dear and have done the same with our country. Some might call it human nature, but no. We *chose* to destroy ourselves.

Still walking as if in a trance, I stepped up to one of the immense creatures. Touching it's wood, feeling the life that was in it. I let a tear fall from me and hit the forest floor, watching it as it went. Then it was soaked up by the Earth, sucked into the roots of the tree to give new life. Something then caught my eye. At the base of the towering behemoth, I saw it, the Cortezeon Plant.

Its pointed leave's browned on the edges, it looked sickly, but there was no mistaking it. At that moment I wanted to tear that organism apart, it had caused all of this. The Cortezeon Plant had destroyed all that I had loved. I didn't want to live forever if it meant my life was poisoned. The life the plant in front of me gave was a cursed life.

Caught up in the beautiful sounds and sights of the world I lived in, I was shocked to hear a loud, horrifying, gut-wrenching scream.

I looked to my right where in a clearing of trees I saw a soldier, one of my own, pointing a gun at a young woman. While the soldier did this, she just lay there in dirty clothes on the ground. I ran over, jumping in front of the gun and forming a barrier between me and the women. "What are you doing?!" I asked in an angry tone.

"Orders," replied the man, who I recognized as Fred Everett. He had been there when Charlie had died. "General said to shoot any locals. I mean, they did try to kill us."

"As your commanding officer, I command you to stand down," I said, helping the woman up to her feet.

"*General's* orders." Then Fred pushed me to the ground, took up his weapon once more, aimed, and shot the woman on the spot as she was running to the cover of the trees.

I watched it in horror. Not a second thought, just the pull of a trigger. Life had been extinguished like one blows out a candle. No longer did we take time to contemplate what to do with life that is in our hands, now we treated people like nothing. Getting rid of them like we would get rid of a piece of trash.

These terrifying events were happening all around me. Multiple shots ringing out in the air, not even a trial for these men, women, and even children. The A.R. was their judge, and the judge had gone mad. I don't care what they said, we were worse than the people we had overcome. Charolette was right, we were the villains.

Some people were just shot, others were pulled to the ground by gravity bombs (one of the only inventions probably from this century), unable to move, completely helpless and yet still shot while they looked up into the barrel of a gun. It was all so horrible, almost incomprehensible. A people hired by the Tahoens, being slaughtered for what they did. They probably had not even had a choice. When the Tahoens came, they had probably been forced like Sam. Their hands tied behind their backs. This war had driven people mad. Because of one speck, thousands would die. Such a big impact for something so small, something most didn't understand.

Through the chaos, I knew I had to do something. Charlie would have. I knew he was good, I knew he was not a monster. Feet away from me, I saw who I was meant to save. A family of five, a mother and four children, yet no husband. The mother, dirty and in tattered clothing, held a baby, while the other three children cowered behind her. They did not look like locals, however.

Like the others, they were about to be shot. A tall, thin man held a gun at the woman's head and was about to pull the trigger. I knew I could not reach them in time, though thankfully I didn't have to. From behind the man, another local, an old man with a white beard had fought back. He was now throwing rocks at multiple soldiers and causing chaos. One of these rocks hit the man preparing to shoot the family and distracted him. And him, like so many others, left their posts and chased the man into the jungle. I laughed at the sight, stones versus guns. David versus Goliath. One man against a country.

I turned my attention back to the family. Noticing their captor had left, they now turned towards me. No one was around; it was just me and the family. They started backing up into a large tree, stopping just as their feet hit the stump. "No! Please don't hurt us!" The mother screamed.

I stopped walking towards them. "No, I'm trying to do the right thing," I said grimly.

"Wh-why?" she asked, still trying to protect her family.

Looking incredibly depressed, I said, "My friend died for a pointless cause, that same cause is why you all are being killed."

The woman sighed, "I've lost things too. My husband. He hasn't returned to me."

"I'm… I'm so sorry. What was his name?" I asked, trying to calm the woman. So much death! Why wouldn't the losses stop.

"His name was Sam," the woman chuckled. "He would always make me laugh. So strong and protective that he tended to frighten people… but he had a sweeter side."

"I knew Sam! He was part of my battalion!" I shouted excitedly. That's when I realized the frightened children looked just like their father.

"Don't act too excited, you should know by now he's a traitor!" Said the woman, a fire in her eyes. She stepped forward firmly and brought her kids with her.

"He said he did it to protect you."

"He mentioned me. He mentioned Sally!?" Said the woman, perking up.

"Yes; he said something about being blackmailed in order to protect his family," I replied.

As if remembering something, Sally's smile turned to a frown of anger "I told him not to worry about us, told him we could protect ourselves. He didn't listen!"

"Maybe," I said, "but he died a hero, he gave his life so that we could all be here. And I plan on using that opportunity to make sure everyone is safe. Besides, heroes are hard to come by now a day."

I heard the voices of men coming up from the forest behind me. "You better be off, if they see you, it won't be pretty," I said, shooing the family away.

"Young man, my husband wasn't the hero, he was just helping to create one." Sally sniffled. "Use that opportunity well."

Hearing people coming up from the brush, I quickly said to Sally, "You can come back with me to camp, I can help you."

Sally shook her head. "No, I know the A.R. Sam betrayed them and they will not let us, his relatives, get away."

And so, the family ran off into the woods, I knew they would not be the last people I helped, I was finally ready to make a difference.

That day I did in fact save many people, waiting until their captor was distracted and then rescuing families, children, and the old. No matter what I did though, I could not save them all. Many of them died right in front of me. I didn't kill anyone that day, but I blame myself for every death.

As I walked through the blood-spattered mud of the jungle back to base camp at the end of the day, it broke my heart to see all the poor people that I was unable to save. Lying dead in the dirt. Not even getting a proper resting place. Though I had a frown on my face, my fellow soldiers seemed not to care. In fact, some were making jokes with each other, laughing and smiling, not caring that thousands had lost their lives.

One spoke to his companion. "Remember when that one ran, tripped and fell. Idiot!"

The other laughed. "Her face! Priceless!"

"I heard some people were helping those jungle rats! They should be hung for their crimes! Traitors!" He snarled.

His friend nodded. "I swear if I ever get a hold of one of those traitors, I'm going to…" he proceeded to cuss me out. He said it as if he wanted me to hear. Wanted me to lash out and reveal myself. I didn't though. Religion was not common, as if with the dying of trees and life people had lost faith. I remembered something though; Jesus had waited until His time had come. I would wait until mine.

Following everyone into one of the many large tents that crowded the jungle, I was packed with everyone else like a sardine. I realized then that this was one of the dining rooms. The space was pretty sad, it had six folding tables with no chairs set up around them, so we all had to stand. It had a leaky roof like the rest of the tents, and also a dirt floor, which unlike the other tents, was pure mud. The only clean part of the room was a stage at the front where none other than the general himself sat, all while we rolled around in the mud like pigs. That's when my sadness turned to rage.

Trudging through the mud, working my way to a condensed table, I continued to stare at the evil man. I had started this mission off with one goal: to make a better life for my son by earning more money. By getting more power. But now, staring at General Myer, I knew that if I ever wanted a good life for my son, I had to stop the country that had slaughtered innocent people. That had no respect for human life. Because if I didn't, people like Timmy would end up in a world full of monsters. I didn't hate the Andy Region; I hated the people who ruled it with malice.

Me and the rest of my soldiers were at the tables for a long time waiting for food. Standing in the cold mud, shivering in the rain. And when food finally came out of a grimy kitchen, we were served strange looking grits and a cup of dirty water. This only fueled my anger though. And I ended up not eating, even though I had not eaten lunch, and my breakfast had been cereal. In fact, that breakfast seemed like days ago.

I had eaten military food before. It had never been good, but until this time, I had not cared. Then something had clicked in me, I had stopped tolerating what was going on. I felt injustice, and I wanted to stop it. What the country was doing here was wrong, what the world was doing was wrong. We served our army like slaves, getting the bare minimum that would keep us going. I was done with this though, and I would make a difference even if our military tried tirelessly to push us down.

I stood there, a grim look on my face, while others ate their share of grits. While others served a corrupt nation without question and would even kill the guilt-free for them. While others listened, I defied. And while I stared off into space, a loud ringing went off in the tent. "Attention, attention everyone," started General Myer, tapping a nice, silver soon against a glass cup filled with red wine. I looked down at my own filthy plastic cup. "Thank you so much for your compliance today. Without you this war could not be, and we intend to win it!" With that remark, many people clapped and cheered towards General Myer, supporting the fact that they had helped murder people today. They were proud of their crimes and would do it all again at just the slightest word. I also noticed the general's food looked to be a large steak on a plate of China. We were cheering for the man who acted like a king and fed us peasants his leftovers. He wasn't even the president, what the president did was probably times worse. It made me sick. The cruel man kept talking, "The government thanks you for your support, though we would like to remind you the war has not been won. Tomorrow we must continue pushing the evil that owns this island out! Only then will we have a fighting chance to be able to take the island of Dewa Ruci!"

I scoffed at Myer; the island we were on was bigger than Dewa Ruci. Why couldn't we just take this one? I knew the answer though, we had become greedy. The country which had started out just wanting freedom now was looking at a bigger goal, world domination. And we would beat and kill anything that stood in our way. But I could feel there was another reason, something I had yet to think of.

I wanted to scream and shout at the mad man which my army followed, to tell him what a monster he was, but I held my tongue. I had to wait until I could help as many people as possible.

Someone, *someone* who had not been brainwashed yet, must have felt the same as me, because from the back of the tent a young woman screamed, "No! No, no, no! It's all wrong, the people on this island were just trying to protect their land, they meant no harm. If you weren't so power hungry, this could all be resolved!"

For a second, I smiled. Happy I wasn't the only one. Then General Myer and the rest of the dining hall noticed this woman. None of their expressions changed, the crowd just stared, and the general continued to smile. Like robots they stared, under the control of a mad master. Finally, the general moved, but all he did was nod towards a dark corner of the tent. Instantaneously two heavily armed soldiers popped out of the shadows, grabbed the girl by the arms, and took her kicking and screaming out of the tent into the night. I could tell she wasn't with us, most likely a rebel. Protesting *our* crimes. Outraged at how the world told us what to do in the worst kind of way. Controlling even what we learned, like the purge of all knowledge relayed to genetic science. Even if it was bad, we and the right to learn about it, to know about it.

The second she had exited, the room turned back to normal. Laughs continued, the warm smiles of friendly faces came back, and of course the generals' speech. In which he talked about the A.R. and its goals. The only thing out of the ordinary were the screams and gunshots which came from outside. Eventually though, those noises stopped, and those two soldiers which had left came back in. This time with blood-stained shirts and faces. They continued to smile though, even when that girl never came back inside. I smiled. It was fake, but I still smiled. Inside though I was crumbling, tearing down the walls of the old me who took orders and rebuilding someone who would fight.

As everyone continued to smile, I was thinking. I wasn't thinking of how I had been lucky I hadn't spoken up, or how that could have been me. I just thought of how I would make these wicked people pay. I would make a difference or at least try to. And even if it was small, it would change things.

I didn't like to kill innocent people, but these people were not innocent.

Chapter 14

The night had ended with a happy crowd, and full

stomachs. Well, that's how everyone else felt at least. I had

gone to bed starving, and angry at the people around me.

And where I slept did not help either. Being forced to sleep

in a sleeping bag, in the mud, and surrounded by my fellow

soldiers.

Well, every soldier except General Myer of course.

The general had slept in a nice, cozy tent,

suspended above ground, out of reach of the wild beasts

which hunted in the evening. Every soldier knew they were

there. Because in the cold of night, when there was no light

except from the moon and the stars (somehow not blocked

by the clouds), you could hear the cries and roars of them.

For everyone it was a new experience, none of us knew

what a jaguar or a wild pig sounded like. We were used to

the loud noises of a bustling metropolis, not a jungle full of animals that wanted to tear us to shreds. The only animals we had ever seen were in pictures or in cages, the last of them went extinct hundreds of years ago with many of the trees. In fact, some of the only animals that had thrived were the massive sea monsters, which lurked in the depths of the ocean, getting bigger and bigger with the radioactive material we had dumped into the sea.

It was strange, sleeping under the stars. At home they were seldom seen, with light pollution and the infinite smog. Here though they shone brightly, hundreds of them. You could see the Milky Way, streaked across the night sky like a painting. From a young age I was obsessed with space. Something about it, seeing thousands of other worlds besides ours. Barely visible yet amazingly beautiful. I had always accepted I was small. was short, and that made it difficult to do stuff. But now I finally realized how small. I went to sleep, questioning where I stood on the scale of the universe.

Yawning, I now took a minute to study the jungle in the new morning light, where there was just enough to see before the sun rose. That's when I noticed how absolutely majestic it was. Between the crashing of the waves, and the morning dew on the branches, the forests would have been wonderful under different circumstances. However, across the forest floor lay the corpses of the fallen, all innocent locals, young and old. Not a single Andy Region soldier laying among them. The scene was enough to make me lurch back, and if I had eaten, I would have thrown up. I stood up off the ground, which seemed like an awful place to be. The bodies of those that had died, lay flat, slowly rotting away in the humid jungle air. In fact, already the forest was starting to claim them. Flies buzzed around them; ants the size of a finger crawled about their resting place. All the while massive, black birds of prey came swooping down from the heavens to peck at the rotting flesh. What I saw made me question my faith in humanity.

We had left our own kind out in the sun and showed no sympathy even to give them a proper burial. Were we even human anymore?

We were monsters, more evil than the foulest of creatures. In our uprising we had lost our home, turning our own planet into a dumpster. And at the same time, we had lost what made us human beings. Our compassion, empathy, and kindness. Our species was a lost one.

Or was it?

There would always be people like me, like the poor woman last night. People like us, who would stand up and remember we could make a difference, even if our numbers were few. In the end, if there were people like us who saved poor families that were like Sam's, we might have a chance. It would take someone who realized the true extent of the human race though. Someone who understood more than any of us.

I walked towards the dining hall, away from the horrors, where some people were starting to gather at the front. I worked my way across the field of sleeping bags which still contained their owners and began to notice something. Every single man and woman just sat there upon opening their eyes. No gasping, no frightened looks, they just sat. Some gave a yawn or two, but many just looked around at their apocalyptic surroundings, and slowly got up.

When I made it to the back of the line, most of the sleeping people had awakened, starting to join me to get food. One of these people happened to be Darlin, who I waved over to get in line with me.

Darlin looked terribly frightened, and held his hands across himself, almost as if to give himself a hug of comfort. Once reaching me, Darlin kind of just stood there, holding himself in an embrace, and slowly rocking back and forth. We stood there for a while, completely silent and only moving when the line occasionally inched forward. At one point though, Darlin broke the silence, and I instantly knew how he felt about yesterday's events. "What they did to those people... it was horrible."

"I know, and that woman from the dining hall... a rebel?"

Darlin nodded. "I did hear there were rebels here, she must have snuck over and..."

We were in silence once more. Both of us were in shock from what had happened, and talking about it only made us hurt more. It was then that I realized why Darlin was so quiet, he must have witnessed things like this before. And if I wanted to help, I needed as much information as I could get. No matter the cost and no matter the pain it caused. "This isn't the first time the government has done this before... or the first time you've seen it happen, is it?" I asked.

"No… And we shouldn't be talking about this, if you don't agree with them, they'll just take you out of the picture."

"I know, but I'd like to know more," I replied, desperate for any new knowledge.

Darlin sighed. "Ever since the Third World War," Darlin started in a whisper, "land has been short, the A.R. needs all the resources it can get. And they'd prefer not to take in more people; the population is already too high. So instead of taking people with the land, they just take the land and kill the inhabitants, making people like Kyle or Myer rich… just like the *plant* made them rich. They always give a reason, like that 'they wanted war,' or 'they were a threat,' but those are all excuses." Darlin shook his head. "There was one family, one family." Darlin was shaking. "They made me do… horrible things. I don't talk much, but I see things. I listen. And the things I've heard have just hardened me."

"But I was stationed in the Taiwan Wars after WWIII, I saw none of this? And though our goal was to take land, I saw us take prisoners," I said, getting curious.

"It all depends on the leader. Some show mercy, while others… well, just look at General Myer," said Darlin.

I looked down at my feet, Darlin was right, it seemed that evil people like them were becoming more common in the world. And it didn't help that the Cortezeon Pill was one of the most valuable things in the world. An easy thing to gain power off of. Could that be it? Was that why we were so desperately driven to take Dewa Ruci? Was capturing Dewa Ruci just another way to profit off of the Pill?

Finally reaching the front of the line, me and Darlin were greeted by a large woman who held a cardboard box full of what was breakfast. Unsurprisingly it was cereal.

"Where is the milk?" I asked the lady as she handed me a box of my small meal.

"There is none."

Walking forward in the mud, me and Darlin looked at each other, obviously thinking the same thing. Though both of us held our tongue. We knew the consequences of someone overhearing us would be fatal. We walked around aimlessly for a while, dragging our feet through the thick clay, slowly enjoying a meal, even if we were given no drink. Everyone else seemed content. Happy to be where they were, me and Darlin though were on an island, separated by what we thought. Some might say we were weird for standing out. Though we could say the others were monsters for what they had done.

The morning went on like this, and just as the sun was starting to rise high above us, disappearing into the clouds, the loud, deep southern voice of General Myer came over the loudspeaker, and anyone who had yet to wake, woke. "Get up soldiers! We got a ten-mile hike ahead of us, and you do not want to be out in the open at night!"

I rolled my eyes; I knew I shouldn't have expected the general to know that we had just slept outside, out in the open at night. He was just another of the world's ignorant fools. Most likely just being told what he wanted to hear from those below him.

From there, the whole camp came alive. Bustling with the many people who had just gotten up and were running to get their breakfast before they had to go. Attempting to get away from the chaos, me and Darlin stepped outside into the dense jungle air, watching as people ran in and out of the tents.

As we stood outside, the clouds drifting over the towering mountains, the rest of my battalion instinctively gathered around me. The other battalions did the same, all until the whole army stood outside. Waiting until finally, General Myer walked out.

"Good morning, everyone," the general shouted into the crowd, his voice amplified by a microphone. Outside thousands upon thousands stood listening. "We have a long journey ahead of us. Our goal is to take control of this island, claiming the land for our people, and then take Dewa Ruci. To do this though, we must take out the last of the locals, and a group of rebel mercenaries protecting them. We have pinpointed their 'stronghold' but are unable to bomb it because it is tucked away in a cave. Therefore, only a ground team is able to capture it. Squad leaders, you will oversee your troops, leading them ahead with Aerial-Choppers. Each is going a different path to flush out any stragglers. Those of you who I have notified will return to-the H.M.S. Franciscan or the A.R.R. Harold."

With that, General Myer gestured towards a stockpile of the large rotating flying saucers, hidden near the forest edge. Each had a pair of blades at the end of them, which were held just in front of the machines on separate spinning wheels and were gleaming in the morning sunlight. Looking at them, I recalled when I had just been a boy, and they had just been invented. At the time, they had been made fun of and had been called, "the flying weed-whacker", only really an important step in history because they harnessed gravity, allowing them to float with ease. (That had been mankind's only development in the recent years. And though a large one, the technology was mostly used for destruction and war). Now though, looking at the thick jungle brush, they seemed handy. Though I also remembered they were the tool used to fell most trees, and looking at the amazing nature before me, it seemed a shame to cut down some of the last ones.

"By the way," the general added, "I've already marked the camp on your G.P.S. Watches. I'll be meeting you there." And with that final remark, the general hopped in one of the Aerial-Choppers with two of his personal guards and sped off.

With the general gone, my whole battalion turned to me for orders. I sighed, "Okay, you heard what General Myer said, everyone follow me."

With my battalion and the rest of the army, I walked towards the saucers, which were hovering off the ground a few feet from the start of the jungle. As I got closer to the ominous machines, I finally realized how big they were. 15 feet in diameter, and 6 feet high (plus how far they were off the ground), they were truly enormous. Silver, with black stripes, a dome lid that covered the top, and two wheels of blades at the front. It really did look like an instrument of war. The Ariel-Chopper made very little sound (the blades were so thin and sharp they cut through the air without a noise), but I knew one wrong move and it could take off your head. The front itself was insane. The long knives arranged like a chainsaw. Able to rotate and turn at different angles to make precise cuts.

Once me and the rest of my crew reached one of the machines, I stood below it, wondering how me and the rest of my men would get in it. The cockpit looked very small and seemed only fit for one. "How are we all supposed to fit in there?" I asked, speaking my mind.

"Only *you* ride it, sir!" Said a man from the crowd behind me.

My eyes widened with surprise; being a leader was not one of my strong skills, and being singled out was even worse. I knew now of course why I had been picked. I had been picked as a pawn to get closer to Charolette. I would do that, I had to, but now I had to lead. Even if some of those I was leading were monsters. Climbing up onto a small flat part of the ship, I slowly worked my way up until I clambered into the cockpit. Looking down at the controls, the glass lid closing above me, I realized it would be easy to fly. It seemed the machine had only a few controls. An on button, and an off button, both on a joystick in the middle for movement.

Closing my eyes and praying for the best, I slowly put my finger down on the button that would start the Aerial-Chopper. Instantly the engine came alive, the blades of the machine slicing through the air. Humming quietly, almost silently, so quiet I could hear the calls of majestic birds. I looked back at my battalion, giving a slight smile to hide my fear. And my crew just looked right back, ready to start a hard and tiring hike uphill.

I gave a quick glance down at my watch, looking to see which way to go, only to remember it was broken. I signaled for Susan to toss one to me. Looking at it, I slowly guided the joystick forward, towards the North side of the island. Jerking towards the canopy, I crept at first, only going as fast as my crew could walk. As I moved, I soon started getting the hang of my Aerial-Chopper, and so were the rest of the sergeants, all of whom, like me, were inching closer and closer to the jungle's edge. A few of the sergeants, upon reaching the forest, sped forward, leaving their crew in the dust. Others, however, kept a steady pace, and went slowly into the jungle. In the end though, everyone had gone from sight. Lost in the dense undergrowth of the forest. Everyone except me.

I hovered there in my ship, stuck at the edge of the jungle, staring straight out into the trees above. I did not want to cut them down, did not want to harm something so precious. Looking at the paths left by the other Aerial-Choppers, I knew I did not want to do that. They had mowed down the plants which stood in their way, leaving nothing but sawdust and dirt in their wake. I did not want to bring my men to General Myer and the natives. I knew if they were to reach him, they would all kill innocent people. I also knew however that if I did not, I would be stuck on this island, unable to help anyone. And still hundreds would die.

And so, taking another deep breath of air, I pushed the joystick forward slowly, destroying the life which was so important to me. I had to be with the locals, helping them when they needed help.

Grimacing as I hit the trees, sending debris flying. I looked down to see my battalion marching forward, all unfazed at the sight in front of them. Seeing this made me feel so very alone, like no one else understood me. Then I noticed Darlin, and Susan, both looking right at me, a look of sorrow and grief on their faces. I had not talked too much to Susan about this topic, but I knew where she stood. She was a good person.

I continued on my path, continuing to head north, up hills, down valleys, and across rivers. For my crew it was not only difficult, but treacherous. They faced off with long, scaly creatures the size of ten men, that I could not name. Paddled across rivers with currents so strong they could easily sweep you away. In the harsh heat they sweat, while I lie cool and comfortable in my aircraft. To me it didn't feel right, and I couldn't help feeling guilty.

But it still felt good, this small possession of superiority. Being better than your fellow man. Maybe that was why General Myer, or Charolette Hive did what they did. The money, the power. Corrupting what they might have been in another time. Giving them the illusion of being large and important when in comparison to the universe they were microscopic.

And then I hated it all. The power, the Cortezeon plant. I cursed the day I had taken that *drug*, and hated even sitting in the cockpit of the machine which I was in. I was being infected. When I flew the Ariel-Chopper I felt better than everyone else. When I took the Cortezeon Pill, I lived forever. So, I then felt like a god. And by thinking that way I became like General Myer, an emotionless monster.

At that point I was ready to launch myself out of the Aerial-Chopper, so that I might not give into the long for power. Though what good would that do? It would harm my crew, making us have to trek through brush in order to make it out of the jungle. It would hinder the few good people. And so, I lie there still, maneuvering my way through the jungle. Not for me, but for my friends. For the world.

On and on we went, working our way up mountains and boulders, climbing higher and higher until eventually I could see through the clouds that the sun was just above the horizon. My crew was getting tired, and the sun was beginning to set. I began to worry we would not be able to make it to the camp. Switching the Aerial-Chopper off, I popped open the lid of my vessel and peered down at my battalion, who stopped with me. "We're almost there," I shouted down, trying to encourage my group.

I turned back to stare down at my chest. I sighed; we still had a while to go. There was no way we could make it to the native base before dark. And even as I thought this, the last bit of light disappeared behind the mountainous terrain. We were in the dark now. Down below I could hear my troop talking, muttering to themselves, and I knew they felt the same way I did. They felt scared. "Keep moving men," I yelled down, stating once more to move forward. This time though, I left my protective dome open. Not only so that I could hear any dangers, but so I could hear my crew's thoughts.

"Don't you think the natives have the perfect chance to attack us now, or the rebels?" Asked a woman.

"Forget the natives, we should be worrying about the wild beasts that live out here," a man replied.

"No, worry about the disease and illnesses, they thrive in these conditions."

I let out a sigh of relief, they were fearful, not angry. And anger can cause much worse things to happen. Luckily though, fear distracted them, as it always does.

We went on much longer, shivering in the now cold air. Eventually though, just as we were nearing our destination, a cry went up that drowned out all the other jungle noises. It was loud and bone chilling; a sound found only in nightmares. The scream a human being gave as they died. Very soon, more screams followed, filling the night with their terror. All of them coming from the direction of the camp we were supposed to be going to.

All heads turned to the sound, and I looked down, signaling my team to be quiet. Hopping out of the Aerial-

Chopper and landing softly. I got low to the ground, working my way up a steep incline where the sound originated from. Slipping on the mud slicked hill. Upon reaching the top, I beckoned my crew up with me. At the top of the hill lie many shrubs and plant growth, though I could tell by the orange gleam which shown off the cliff face above, that something was up.

Peering through the bushes in front of me, I saw what I had expected. There was the native camp we had been searching for, the only problem was that General Myer hadn't captured the natives, they had captured him. Off the gleam of a small fire, that burned brightly, I could make out a group of people holding guns and spears, ancient compared to our weaponry. They were sitting and watching their struggling captives. Most of the captors were natives, but thrown into the group I could see rebels, in their standard blue uniform, stern looks on their faces. Hanging from a rope tied to an overhanging rock like a spider's caught prey, was the general himself. With him were also about fifteen men, less than I had expected. Only a fraction of a battalion. The rest were nowhere to be seen.

For a while this was how the scene went as we waited for our chance. That was until General Myer's eyes widened, and he looked right at me with a happy grin on his face. Noticing this, one of the locals yelled at a large man who got up off the ground and marched over to the general.

Screaming at him in a language unrecognizable to me, and also to the general, who simply replied in a shaking voice, "I'm sorry, I... I don't understand." And with the slap of his hand, the large man hit the general across the face. "Now listen here, do you know who I am!" Snapped General Myer.

Not caring, the large man proceeded to take a large knife from his pocket and cut the rope which held the general. I watched as General Myer was laid down on the dirt right in front of me, and right beside the corpses of my fellow Andy soldiers.

Startled at the sight of the bodies, which I had not seen because of the concealing darkness, I almost screamed, which would have only blown my cover and sent me to the same fate as the others. If we wanted to help, we needed to use the element of surprise. In the eerie glow of the fire, shadows dancing off the stone wall, the man raised his knife, ready to take the life of the general, and let his screams join those of the others. Part of me wanted this to happen, watch General Myer die for his crimes. But I needed him. I knew there was something on Dewa Ruci he wasn't telling me about. Something sinister that I had to stop, and without his knowledge, and his ride off the island, I couldn't save anyone. Not the rebels, not the natives, not even General Myer's own convoy. With him dead, others would still want the "enemy" killed.

In any group, there would always be one person

who knew what was right and wanted to stand up for it.

The natives and rebels just killed because they were afraid.

I would still save them all, and if that meant saving an evil

man, then I must. And if somehow, someway, I could save

everyone, then everything would be perfect.

Just as the man raised his blade, ready to take the

generals life, I turned back towards my battalion, and

screamed, "Attack!"

Instantly, shots rang out from all around me, most

going towards the large native, yet others being shot at

anything that moved. Men and women screamed from all

directions, howling out as bullets whizzed by their heads. I

did not fire a single shot. Stepping out from behind the

bush, I went towards General Myer, who was lying on the

ground curled in a tight ball. Next to him lie the native,

who sat in a pool of blood. I put my hand on the general,

who instantly sat up. "Oh," he laughed, "thank you Mr. Watson."

"No problem, sir," I replied, lending my hand to the general.

The second the man was up on his feet; he instantly started yelling orders at people to continue fire. Bullets rained terror down upon everyone, and very slowly the locals and rebels were backed up against the cave wall.

At that point, the gunfire had stopped, and the natives had surrendered. The general laughed again, "Excellent! Now we can make these monsters pay for their crimes."

"Are you sure sir, I mean they did surrender?"

"Nonsense, they killed half my men! Those are crimes that must be paid for!" Yelled the general.

"Yes, well we did kill their families," I said through gritted teeth.

"My God, Brian! By the way you talk I'd say you were on their side!" With that remark, the mad man then grabbed my gun from me and pointed it at the defenseless people who were cowering in the corner. "If you won't do it, I will. Men at the ready!"

Many of my men picked up their weapons, ready to fire and kill at just one word. "You can't do this!" I shouted, jumping in front of the general's gun

"Brian, I don't think you get it, we *need* Dewa Ruci. And I don't need your help to take it."

General Myer shoved me aside into a crowd of my own soldiers, I was held back by two large men who made sure their grip was tight. "Don't do this!"

"I'm sorry Brian, but I need to. You don't understand what is riding on Dewa Ruci," said the general. He turned to one of my men and said, "Fire."

The barrage of gunfire was sent towards those people tucked away in the caves. The sound was deafening, and I cried while sagging in my captors' arms. Cried while they all died. Innocent, and people whose beliefs I agreed with. For if this was what the Cortezeon Pill had done to us, it should be destroyed. I cried while Susan and Darlin held their guns up but did not pull the trigger. I cried while General Myer succeeded. But I wouldn't let him win, not yet at least. Cried while the world seemed to fade from around me, as hope almost left my soul.

I needed to find out what that evil man wanted with Dewa Ruci though, because whatever he wanted had to be terrible. And so, when the firing had ceased, and General Myer was panting, and holding his gun at his side, I looked up at him and said, "You won't win. Whatever it is you want with that stupid island, I'll make sure you never get it."

But the general just looked at me and frowned, saying, "If only you knew what was on that rock."

"So, tell me," I said. "Tell me and maybe I'll understand."

He shook his head. "It's too important," said General Myer. "You'll know soon enough though."

Saying this, the general took a deep breath and shoved the butt of the gun into my face with all his strength. I blacked out. Slipping to the ground with the rest of the fallen.

Chapter 15

I awoke with a deep throbbing in my head, and the smell of rain and a strong coffee brewing. I first opened my eyes, the outside light, though muffled by clouds, blinding me. I had a splitting headache, and as I slowly sat up, dots began to dance in my head. I put my hand down to catch myself, finding that I was on a dirty floor, with tattered cloth covering me.

My eyes were now adjusted so I looked around, trying to figure out what had happened after I had been hit, vaguely remembering being knocked out. I was in a rock cavern, tucked away behind a stalagmite that rested on the ground. I wasn't too far from the outside, and could see that it was once again raining, and that a dense fog covered the land. Beside me was a small fire where a pot filled with what I assumed to be the coffee, roasted.

Instantly coming to my senses, there was no doubt in my mind that I had to get to General Myer. Had to stop him, the A.R., and anyone else who was taking advantage of the world. I threw off the sheet covering me and tried to jump up only to get lightheaded and fall over. I landed on one of the many rocks which littered the cavern floor. When I looked down the rock was covered with blood. But checking my hand I saw it was unscathed.

It was then that I knew exactly where I was, the same cave where Myer had murdered all those people. Now with a little bit more awareness, I saw that the cave had blood all over it, yet not a single body.

Why did we have to murder? Why did we have to kill? All I wanted to do was go up to President Kyle's and General Myer's smug face and ask him why they had decided to let us kill for that one island. They both had allowed us to take people's dreams, their lives, their families. So, what was on that rock that needed this much sacrifice? Humans are small, but our lives aren't pointless, each person has a purpose.

I looked around myself once more. Someone here had a purpose, saving me from whatever fate I might have faced otherwise. I doubted the general had put me in this cave, so who had? Someone had decided to help another human being. Why couldn't everyone do that? Was it because we thought of ourselves too highly? Did we believe that we were too important to help the needy? Like the streets of the city, if you fell you would be trampled. But why?

I soon heard footsteps approaching though, my rescuer returning most likely. I fell back to the ground, putting my blanket back over myself, pretending to be asleep. I faced the other way, just listening to the sounds of whoever was coming. I could hear the sound of feat entering, moving close to me, and tending to the fire. Picking up the pot from the flame and pouring the liquid into a cup. I heard something slide toward me, and then a male voice said, "I know you're awake, there is no need to pretend to sleep. You've been out long enough, at least a day and a half."

I turned around slowly, sitting up but keeping the blanket over my knees. I then set eyes on the man, hesitating to look him in the eyes. He had a mop of blonde hair, splattered with mud just like the blue uniform he wore. He had a tall build, with a thick neck which the collar of his shirt covered, and very pale skin. His uniform was a baby blue jumpsuit, with two white stripes running down it all the way down to his feet. "You're… a rebel," I gasped. Part in awe but also fear for the stories I had heard of the mercenaries.

He chuckled. "Yea, I am."

Almost uncontrollably, I asked, "You're not going to kill me, are you?"

Again, he laughed. "No," he said. "Rebels don't do that, or at least all the rebels I know. That's all government propaganda. We don't want to kill people; we just want to make the world a better place."

Taking a second to review what was being said, trying to figure out if I was being lied to, I said, "But my friend said her family was killed by…"

He shook his head saying, "It's horrible what they do, they take people who have died in an air taxi accident or something and blame it on us. You can believe me or them, but I saw what your general did to you. We just don't take the Cortezeon Pill. Occasionally we fight the government, but we don't harm civilians."

"So… how old are you?"

"45."

I looked the man up and down once more. He looked almost the same age as me, yet I was ancient compared to him. Accepting what he had said, I asked, "What happened?"

"He knocked you out, left you for dead. You're lucky I found you; it got cold last night."

"How did you find me?"

My protector let out a deep sigh, shuddering. "I was one of the rebels you all attacked. The only reason I survived was by hiding behind the… bodies. I'm the only survivor."

Upon saying this, I saw that the rebels weren't the monsters they had been worked up to be. If anything, they were more human than us. I glanced down at the dark liquid, which was in a cup at my feet, feeling how dry my throat was. "Drink some," he said.

Trustingly, I picked up the steaming cup and sipped it slowly. It was a dark coffee and filled me with much-needed energy. "What's your name?" I asked.

"Beau Everette. You?"

"Brian Watson. Why'd you save me?"

Beau shrugged. "I saw what you did for us; you seemed like you deserved it. Besides, there's already too much death."

We sat for a while, warming ourselves with our drink. I saw now in full, how horrible the Andy Region had become. Making it seem as if a group of people fighting for the good of the world was evil. Just so they could sell a drug to everyone. And now they were murdering for an island. But an island with what on it? I turned to Beau. "I'd like to see the bodies."

Beau nodded sympathetically, unquestioningly, and led me outside into the mist which covered the outside. The ground was charred, and a small burn area could be seen reaching slightly into the forest. "They killed everyone and left, along with starting a few fires. Their carrier is off the coast somewhere, heading to Dewa Ruci. But your General shouldn't be there yet. He's probably still on the island."

All around me were the dead, rebels and locals alike. Resting in the dirt side by side. The only reason they were even facing up was because Beau had wanted to at least try to respect them. The rows of men covered almost all the open terrain. There were at least a hundred corpses, so much death caused by the actions of one man. So much horror. Yet I didn't cry this time, because I knew what was done was done. But that didn't make it right. Now it was time to make a difference. "You know about Dewa Ruci?" I asked Beau. He nodded. I walked up to him, still trying to hold back tears, stuttering as I spoke. "What... what do you know?"

"Why do *you* want to know?" Beau asked curiously.

"That monster, and anyone else who believes *this* is right, needs to be stopped." I pointed at the bodies as I spoke.

Beau smiled. "Follow me."

We stepped back into our hide away, and away from the outside terrors. The fire was slowly going out, and I saw it as what was happening to my own species. We had once been a strong, blazing flame. Now we were failing. As a fire uses up any fuel to keep itself alive, we were destroying ourselves just like that. Taking resource after resource. Oil, wood, land... even life. We took until there was nothing more to take and then suffocated in our own design. Like the fire.

Beau crawled over to a small bag and opened it, removing a rolled-up piece of paper and a small recording device. He put the paper to the side but set the recording device high on a rock ledge. Pushing play, Beau signaled for me to listen.

Some static went through, but soon a young, female voice spoke quick and panicky. *"General Myer, this is Dr, Wendell. I have continued the research requested on the Cortezeon Plant and I am truly worried. As I had previously suspected, the plant is dying. But not on the scale either of us thought. Within a decade it will become extinct. The Farm system isn't even helping; the plant is still not surviving in our modern conditions. We have made the soil and water so acidic that no amount of filtering can prevent what is coming. We both know the fate of the new world is riding on the survival of the Cortezeon Plant. I suggest you lead an expedition to Farm Outpost 1; it should be exposed now. Though I have heard that others may be going after it for the same reason. The A.R. and mankind depends on you, good luck."* Back to static.

Beau clicked the recording off. "We intercepted that message last week, along with others like it which were going to almost every world powerhouse," he spoke.

I looked awestruck at the rebel. "Farm Outpost 1 isn't…" I started.

Beau nodded. "Dewa Ruci."

I tried to sit down, feeling dizzy again. The Cortezeon Plant, gone?! It was hard to believe, yet in a way I had always known it to be true. We had indeed destroyed ourselves. Just not in the way I had thought we would. Not on that scale. And if the plant did cease to exist, maybe that would be for the best. "So, what is on Dewa Ruci?" I asked.

Grabbing the rolled-up sheet, Beau straightened it out and placed it next to the dying fire so we could see it clearly. "This," he said, "is a schematic of Dewa Ruci, or Farm Outpost 1. From the information we have gathered it was built right around the same time the Cortezeon Plant was found. It was almost 200 feet above sea level, but with rising ocean levels it had been submerged as the recording stated. Our ancestors wanted to make sure that if anything went wrong, and the human species was fading, that we had something to boost our population." Beau gestured towards the schematic which showed a drawing of Dewa Ruci except that it clearly showed the door I had seen and also gave a clear view of what was under the water. From the door, which was on the surface, an elevator shaft ran down deep into the Earth's crust, until it finally hit a small chamber. There, branches of rooms ran around like a maze. Pointing to the rooms Beau said, "One of those is where we believe they keep a Cortezeon Plant, cut off from the rest of the world. But it's special, apparently, it's a different breed. Created by genetic scientists before the destruction and ban of that specific field. Before the XG-971 virus. And if our intelligence is to be believed, it was specifically modified to survive the harshest conditions. If anyone gets it, the plant will start a new generation of marketing and taking of the Cortezeon Plant. That's why we all want to be the first to get it.

My mouth dropped. "They killed all the people out there for money," I whispered.

"Yes, and we were planning on stopping anyone from getting to Dewa Ruci. We were planning on ending the madness. Sending a raid to San Francisco, we tried to distract the A.R., setting up multiple missile launchers here, and making calculations to hit the island in just a way that we could destroy what might soon be the last Cortezeon Plant. And without any bioengineering knowledge, the species would never be able to be duplicated. Not only would the Earth return to its natural glory, but the A.R. and the rest of those horrible countries would fail without the Plant's economy to profit off of. But then the war for Dewa Ruci came here, and General Myer found out about our plans. He destroyed our only chance to save the planet. Now every nation is heading to Dewa Ruci, ready to profit off the destruction of the beautiful world which is almost fully gone."

I sat back on the hard, stone floor, pondering all of this new information. I didn't even care that Beau had been part of the attack on the Bay Area. I just kept thinking of the same thing: how they had been so close. The rebels had almost stopped everyone. If they had succeeded, and the last Cortezeon Plant had died, maybe the world would have returned to the state everyone longed for. But no, we had lost what might have been our last chance. Destroyed Timmy's future. I looked at Beau solemnly. He didn't seem to care that I had ruined what he believed in, maybe even gotten his friends killed. "Is there anything we can do."

Tapping the schematic of Dewa Ruci, Beau said, "Destroy that plant."

"How?" I asked. "Your whole rebellion couldn't even do it."

Beau nodded. "Maybe not, but we give it one more try. Not for us, but for our children. Our children's children, for the generations in the future that might be able to see a better world than the one we see today." Beau stuck out his hand. "One last try?"

I stared down at the blazing fire. All for Timmy. I grabbed the man's hand, shaking it. "Let's do it."

Smiling, Beau asked, "So how do we do it?"

"You know the island, I know the A.R." I laughed, saying, "It was about time I did something."

. . .

Me and Beau walked side by side in the sweltering, afternoon heat of the jungle. We had been hiking across the harsh terrain for almost an hour now and had barely spoken to each other. But that was expected, both of us were too focused on reviewing every step of our plan. Making sure it went flawless.

The sweat dripped down from me was dirty and bloody, and soon we were sitting on a small rock next to a creek getting a drink and catching our breath. "How much longer?" I asked.

Beau looked down at his compass, then at the surrounding environment. "I'd say about another half hour before we get to General Myer. He took the long way to get to the rendezvous for their carrier. We should be close."

I turned to stare at the nature around me, slowly sipping from my canteen. The jungle was dense here, and small birds hopped down from the greenery occasionally to drink from the stream. And all-around flowers floated down to me in the wind. It was truly amazing, making me long for the cabin on the hill. And that was why our plan had to work. So, we could keep all of what was in front of me. So I could get more. Beau must have been thinking the same thing, because as he was watching the flowing waters he asked, "Do you think it'll work, I mean what happens if something goes wrong, or if… we fail. All the dead men… they would have died for nothing."

I turned back to Beau, his rebel uniform wet from the humid climate. "Then we fail. Maybe things won't be as good as we want them, but we'll still be here. We are insignificant compared to the universe, and this moment is of even less importance. To a universe which has been around for billions of years, what happens next means nothing. We've just made it seem as though it is of highest importance," I said.

"That's a dark outlook."

"Yea," I sighed, "but it's true."

I didn't say it, but all I could think about was that even if this moment didn't matter compared to other things, it needed to succeed. At least in my eyes, someone who didn't have a view of the whole universe, it needed to work. Because I only had one rock, and that was all that mattered to me. Taking another swig from his canteen, Beau asked, "But you do think we can do it?"

"If we ever had a chance, this is it," I said while putting my own water away.

We gathered our things and began hiking again, crossing the steam and working our way down to the beach opposite where we came in. There, we would hopefully find the general, and our scheme would begin.

It was all downhill from the creek, and though at first this was a pleasant difference from the uphill battle we had previously fought, it soon became extremely steep. At some places the damp earth even dropped off into large ravines, filled with thick brush. And when we weren't dealing with the drop-offs, we'd have to navigate through the impossible layers of trees. Beau had a machete which he used to hack away thinner trees, but I had to follow behind, and it took a long time to clear a path. It hurt me every time Beau swung his blade. When I walked by the chopped wood and destroyed leaves of plants I could only think about how if I didn't move, it would all be gone.

Soon, we came out of the dark forest and onto a cliff edge. The sun shining on us only slightly, blocked off by more clouds. The cliff was high above the sandy beaches below, where the sea rolled against them softly. Offshore was the aircraft carrier, the A.R.R. Herald, and even farther out in the ocean there would be more battleships, all heading towards Farm Outpost 1. On the golden sand underneath us, small boats were docked with men slowly loading into them. It was the general, we had caught up to him.

Beau stepped away from the cliff, kneeling on the rocky outcropping. "Let's go over the plan one more time," he said, taking off his backpack and digging through it.

I got away from the edge of the bluff and sat beside Beau as he removed a small inflatable raft, and then a small capsule no bigger than my hand, it was the corner stone of our master plan. It was an F.E.D., a Foam Explosive Device. An explosive which was easy to attach to any surface but rarely distributed to the Andy Region's military. Beau handed me the F.E.D. and then resealed his backpack. I held my thumb on the trigger of the small capsule and then holstered it to my belt. "Okay," said Beau, "you have the F.E.D., and you're sure you know how to use it?"

"Yes," I replied.

"Because I'll have one too, but the hull can only be broken from the inside, and even then, only at the location we discussed. And you still think General Myer won't kill you on the spot?"

I shook my head. "Trust me, I have a plan."

Beau shrugged, putting away the raft, standing back up to peer over the cliff face once more. I followed and put my hand on the back of his blue jumpsuit. "I should go now," I said.

"Brian, you don't have to do this if you don't want to… No one's making you." Beau said. And in his voice, I heard sadness. Authentic saddens for someone he had just met. Someone who had helped slaughter his people.

Replying, I said, "I'm making myself."

And I walked off, leaving Beau on the rock ledge to watch me work my way to the beach. He would study me from afar, waiting until the next phase of our plan was ready to go into effect. If all went well, I would be seeing him when it was time for us to get our revenge.

I hiked down the cliff edge, grabbing vines to support myself on the steep hillside. I had to be quick in order to get to the army on time. Perspiration dripped down my neck, and mosquitoes bit at my bleeding skin but none of it mattered. I had to get to Dewa Ruci, I had to make the world beautiful again.

We would always endure. We wouldn't die. Yet all of us would wish we were dead. At worst we would just colonize another planet, and like a disease we would destroy it. The greenery, the beauty... it wasn't necessary. But I don't know if it was worth living without. The zoo would always be with us, just so we could feel as if we hadn't ruined our lives. However, just like a plant that pushes off death, it was all an illusion. No matter how long you could live, if the world around you was hideous, it might not be worth living in.

I pushed aside a drooping palm branch, wet with morning dew, and stepped out onto the beach. Walking a couple of steps out from under the foliage with no fear, my feet sinking into the sand, I trudged over to General Myer and company. They were picking up large crates and loading them onto the small boats. And even from a couple hundred yards away, I could hear the General screaming at his troops. "Faster!" He shouted. "Every country is heading right at Dewa Ruci. We must be the first ones to that island!"

A little closer to myself, men were sprawled on the ground in rebel uniforms. Gasping for air as one by one a man with gun would walk by and shoot them with a pistol. I could hear the shots ring out, see the rebel's bloody corpses laying in pools of blood, but all around me people didn't seem to notice. They went on packing up. But as I was walking through these horrific scenes, I saw two people who weren't helping. Two people who just sat and tried not to sob.

Susan was sitting on a crate, resting her hand on Darlin who was below her. My heart jumped when I saw the both of them. How happy I was that they were safe. Darlin met my eyes first, and I could see him mutter under his breath, "My God."

Susan heard him and looked in my direction, her eyes lighting up when she saw me. Others, (some of my own crew members) saw the commotion and dropped what they were doing to stare at me. A ragged figure with a bleeding head and torn clothes. General Myer also saw me, and when he did, I could see the cruel man shake his head in disbelief.

He began walking towards me, whistling to call over some of his henchmen. The general stopped 10 yards from me, with soldiers surrounding me in a circle. Their weapons pointed directly at my face. Putting my hands in the air, I watched Susan come running over to me. Only to be stopped by more soldiers.

"I'm sorry," she mouthed. Her eyes filled with tears.

I could tell how desperate she was to help, and how upset she was that she couldn't. That was good. As cruel as it sounded, I needed her and Darlin in order to fulfill our plan. Without the two of them our scheme would fail right out of the gate. "Mr. Watson," said General Myer. I noted how he didn't call me *sergeant* and then continued to listen. "You aren't dead."

"What can I say," I scoffed, "I'm a fighter."

The general chuckled slightly. "Those two," he said pointing towards my friends, "were extremely worried about you. You're lucky I didn't blow their heads in, just like I'm about to do to you."

The men around me inched closer. I could see right through the general though. Trying to scare me, it wouldn't work. I looked sternly at General Myer. It was time. I said,

"I killed the rest of them. The rebels that is. You missed a few."

Susan covered her mouth to stop a gasp, and I could tell that what I had said had had an influence on the general. I also knew that above me Beau watched like my guardian angel. He would have noted the ripple which went through the people surrounding me. General Myer seemed truly surprised, saying, "Why... why would you do that?"

The men around me still had their weapons aimed at me, but I could already tell that I was in. I put my hands down, laughing. "I know what's on Dewa Ruci, or should I say: Farm Outpost 1," I said.

Muttering flowed throughout the army. No one knew what was in Dewa Ruci, and now a *traitor* knew. *Why weren't we allowed to know?* That was what they asked themselves. That was good, unrest weakened a fighting force. They now had doubts about their leaders.

The general put his hand up, quieting everyone down, and signaling his soldiers to put their guns away. They obeyed instantly, but stayed tense, not moving from the ring which surrounded me. Puzzled, General Myer asked, "How?"

I had him! He had fallen into my trap perfectly. "After eliminating any *stragglers* that you left behind, I found some of the *rebel scum's* plans," I said. "I'm well aware of why you had to do what you did. And now I know. We must get Dewa Ruci."

I could see the General pondering what I had said, reviewing his options. However, he had none. Killing me would just create trouble. Too many people would begin asking why knowing what was on Dewa Ruci was worthy of death. At the same time, if he didn't kill me, it would teach people that fighting for Farm Outpost 1 was a fight they wanted to be a part of. For if a turncoat had repented with his army after finding out about Dewa Ruci, then it must be a just cause. General Myer saw this too, and nodded, saying, "Okay Brian. I can see you've seen the error of your ways." Turning to the troopers, he snapped, "Cuff him and strip him of his gear. We'll put him in a cell on the A.R.R Harold. He still betrayed us, and that is unforgivable."

A large woman came up to me and put me in yet another set of sterolined cuffs, taking my bag and peering in it and finding the F.E.D. She gave it a funny look, wondering why I had such a device, but put it away and threw the bag to one of her fellow soldiers.

There was some slight turmoil in the crowd, I could see that. Some people giving the general a puzzled look for his decision, but soon it subsided, and people continued getting ready for departure as if nothing had happened. The woman pulled sharply at my cuffs and lead me over to a boat. She half dragged me there, and when I was sitting down, I couldn't help searching for Susan's face.

I found her, alongside Darlin, fighting against guards, which made sure my boat had a chance to leave the amazing island. Leave the last good place on the planet. Susan sobbed and kicked up sand every time she attempted to lunge over the soldiers. Darlin pushed and shoved at them as well. And oh, how I longed to be with them. Fighting the corruption which had destroyed our planet.

But though I wasn't chained to my small boat, I didn't attempt to hop out. My friends were probably wondering why I didn't try. The boats had soon all left shore, and nothing would help. My plan was working, that was all I could think about. And even if all was working, I shed so many tears.

Susan would need to help me. Sweet, lovely Susan. You would need to make some hard choices in the near future. Along with Darlin. I laughed in between my sobs; Darlin would have to do some things he may have never done before.

The waves were big and crashed over the bow occasionally. Spraying me with water. Water, which was once salty, and if all went well, would be salty once more. I looked back at the island which was becoming distant now. Its greenery was beginning to fade. Smoke filled the air around it, and you could see human structure slowly taking over, overcoming the beauty. Like it had done to the rest of the planet.

I thought I saw a figure standing in the smoke-filled hills. Beau, standing and waving me off. That was a good man. If only there were more like him.

Chapter 16

The A.R.R. Harold rocked back and forth with the hit of each massive wave. Despite its size, the waves still had a large effect on the vessel. With each one washing over the ship causing anything not bolted down to slide about.

I, of course, was unable to even glance at the towering walls of water. In fact, I only knew the size of the A.R.R Harold from what I had seen upon boarding. I was hoisted up onto the ship from my smaller transport, my handcuffs removed, and then instantly pushed and shoved into a small prison cell. A one room jail with the only furniture being a small desk on the other side of my bars upon which my gear was laid out. The bars not only kept me from my gear, but also from causing problems.

And at the moment, I knew the general was having enough trouble. I stood in my cell, holding on to the bars, trying not to fall with the turmoil the ship was in. Besides the ominous waves, the shaking of a large bomb or torpedo exploding occasionally caused dust to come fluttering down from the metal ceiling.

That was how I knew we had arrived at Dewa Ruci. Finally, after the rush to the island, every nation aware of this last Cortezeon Plant had converged. Unleashing one of the most epic battles in naval history upon the sea. What happened now would change the future. For better or worse. It was the end game; all I needed now was to wait. Wait for my chance. Because once I started, there would be no turning back. The small decisions I made now would unleash a tidal wave of events that would determine what kind of world Tim grew up in.

It only helped my cause that General Myer had been careless about leaving my equipment out, along with no guards for what I could tell. There could be some outside of my small room, but it didn't matter. Or at least that was what I kept telling myself. Backstage, behind my hope, with every second that went by, my stress built. What if I couldn't get out of my jail? What if I failed Beau? What if I was stuck here while the A.R. sealed the world's awful fate? If that were to happen, I don't know if I could live with myself. The only thing that kept me sane at this moment was by lying to myself and saying it didn't matter.

However, if I knew Susan and Darlin, if I knew my friends, then they would have help. I wouldn't have to face my hardships alone. It wouldn't just be one small person against the world; I would have others.

And so, I stood still as the bombs went off. As a battle raged overhead. As men died for a cause they didn't even know the proportions of. All I could do was stare at my backpack which held the F.E.D. I wanted to lunge for it and begin the battle I had always wanted to fight. In a way, ever since the beginning I had always longed to change what I saw as a horrible world. Always that voice in my

325

head whispered and told me that what was in front of me was not right. But the A.R. had just deafened that voice by screaming at me their phrase:

"The Andy Region controls everything. The Cortezeon Plant is money. Money is power. Power fuels innovation. To gain wealth, we must conquer anyone and anything around us. Anyone or anything who stands against our conquest is the enemy. Do not sympathize with the enemy. The enemy prevents you from getting money. Money is power…"

Now I realized the stupidity of that chant though. Yes, they told you how to get power, but what they didn't tell you was at what price that power would come. Monopolizing a drug was not worth any amount of power. That was I was going to fight now.

Susan and Darlin burst into my prison at the same time. Both were panting hard and fought for balance on the moving floor. "Brian!" Susan screamed, running up to my *cage*. Grabbing my hands from the other side and squeezing hard.

She was here! My spirits were lifted high with the sight of her. She had come for me. She cared for me. She would help me make a difference.

Darlin was close behind her, coming up to me and grabbing at the iron bars. "You all right Mr. Watson?" He asked.

I looked away from Susan for a moment. "Yes, I'm all right," I replied. I was far too happy to say anything else.

After hearing this, both Darlin and Susan let go of my cell and looked at each other awkwardly. Something unspoken preventing any further action. They looked at me now as if I had done something horrid. As if I was no longer the man they had known. Darlin cleared his throat, glancing towards me with darting eyes. "Brian," he said skittishly, "did... you really kill those rebels?"

It was a legitimate question, and even though it was a common misunderstanding, it hurt me that someone even thought I was capable of such a thing. But I shrugged it off, because now there were more important matters to attend. I scoffed, exclaiming, "God no!"

Confused, Darlin probed, "Then... what did you do?"

I glanced around anxiously. Tapping my foot faster and faster with every moment. Beau needed me, I didn't have time to answer questions. I ignored what Darlin asked completely, but instead looked him right in the eyes, desperate to get out of prison. "Darlin, what time is it?"

Darlin looked down at his watch, but before he could speak, Susan answered for him. "It's almost eight now."

She had been looking through my bag, and was now holding the F.E.D. Her other hand on her hip. "These are rebel explosives. What did you do Brian?" Susan questioned angrily.

Knowing she wanted the truth, I clenched my fists even tighter around the metal bars. It was already eight! I didn't have the time, Beau needed me!

I turned to face Susan. Her eyes were melancholy, hurt from the fact that I might have done something truly horrible. She liked that I didn't want to kill. Didn't want to hurt people. But that was why I needed to get out, so that I could save people from a danger they didn't know they were in. I said, "Susan, I want to tell you, but we need to hurry. I did lie about killing those poor souls on that island, but I didn't lie about finding out about Dewa Ruci. And now I need you."

A blast shook the ship, dislodging dirt from above. Turmoil covered Susan's face. Unsure, she looked at Darlin. But he just shook his head. A good man but scared so badly from the disgusting society we lived in that he no longer wanted to take a chance. Even if he could make a difference.

"Darlin, give me your gun." Susan demanded.

"Susan, are you sure…"

Susan grunted. "Darlin, just give it to me."

Reluctantly, Darlin passed his pistol over to Susan's open palm. "Stand back," she told me.

As I did, I began to calm Darlin's concerns about me. "Darlin," I said, "you'll understand soon enough. And when you do, you'll get why I'm in such a rush."

Darlin nodded but still seemed nervous about what he was doing. I *would* tell him though. Because in the world we lived in, one so full of bad people, it was good to have friends you could trust.

Susan held the gun firmly; its barrel pointed at the lock of my prison cell. I was backed in the corner, crouched with my hands over my head. She pulled the trigger, and with an exclaiming crack, the door swung open. Fragments of metal lay across the floor, the remnants of what had been the lock. I ran across the shards of metal, my boots crushing the smaller ones, and gave Susan a huge embrace. We held each other in our arms for what seemed like hours. Sharing that one warm moment. I knew she had doubts about me, but I also knew she didn't care. So, we were interlocked for that long time, and even if we didn't have time, it was worth it. Not wanting to, I let go of her and walked over to my bag. Slinging it onto a shoulder and stopping to stare at my friends. I was so happy to see them, so overjoyed. But I still couldn't help grieving for the ones I had lost. Charlie, my wife Kate. If only they could share this moment with me. Help fight beside me for that better world I wanted to create.

Looking between the two of them, I said, "Come with me."

We walked out of the room swiftly, not waiting a second. Susan followed me close behind, but Darlin lingered. He was watching our backs, making sure we weren't being followed. And since Susan had handed me his gun, I couldn't blame him for being nervous. I held the weapon close to me, rounding corners with care.

Of course, according to Susan, almost no one was walking around the ship. And no one was coming to check on me. It was too chaotic on deck. The Rohans and Tahoens were both here, along with Charolette Hive. No one had even touched Dewa Ruci though, that battle was too fierce to leave the seductive "safety" of the vessel.

Darlin and Susan were also both desperate to get answers out of me, so, as were snaking our way to the port side of the A.R.R Harold as me and Beau had discussed, I explained. Explained how I had been rescued by a rebel, how I had learned how they aren't monsters that kill to save, and how I had discovered the truth about Dewa Ruci. Just like me, all this news was incredibly shocking, but when I told them what I wanted to do to that last Cortezeon Plant, they seemed to agree with me. Because just like me, they had seen what life could be like when they had seen that island. The beauty, the growth, all of it they fathomed would be destroyed. But they knew that we could do something. That was why we connected.

Darlin seemed to understand now and recognized what I wanted to do. And along with Susan they wanted to help me make sure that there could be a better world. So, I told them how they could help, and the plan we had to change the world. They agreed to it and promised to do

333

their parts. However, Susan still had one thing to ask. "Brian, after all that, how did you know I would rescue you?"

She realized now that it had been my goal to get captured, so that I might be close enough to let Beau on the ship. That meant she also knew that I had planned for her to let me out. She just didn't understand why I could have so much faith in her. Because faith in the modern world was scarce. You trusted yourself and no one else. So why *had* I believed in her?

Chuckling, I replied, "I don't know. It's just I trust you. With my life. You're a good person, and I know that."

Susan nodded, and we were both quiet for a while.

My wife would want this, that was all I kept telling myself. Kate wanted me to be happy, and the girl next to me made me happy. I also felt that she wanted to do what she was doing. She was just following me to follow me; she was doing what she was doing in because she agreed with the cause. A cause which might not be perfect. A cause which might get her killed. But like me she longed for a world that had been. A lost world.

We came to a fork in the hallway we had been following, where it split off to a staircase which would lead up to the control center. I turned back to Darlin. He nodded and went off to the staircase. None of us wanted to say anything, knowing that after this everything would change… one way or another.

As a technician, Darlin would try to hack into the ship's weaponry from the control room, clearing anyone out in it, and waiting for Beau to direct him on how to destroy Dewa Ruci. Just like Beau had been trying to do. He had always been like me as well. I could see that now. Hating the injustice in the world, wanting to stop it but not knowing how. Now he would help though, he had been bottling up rage for too long. He was ready to unleash his wrath and purge all that had corrupted a once beautiful Earth.

In a way, I think everyone wanted something else. No matter how cruel, no matter how evil, no matter how destructive, no matter who a person was, they didn't want to see a concrete jungle. They just wanted to see a beautiful planet. I refused to think anything else. And anyone who believes for one second that even someone like General Myer is pure monster, and wants a planet empty of life, they are the real demons. Think of people with the upmost grace. Only then can you love the world.

I recalled what Susan had said when I told her about Beau. Her agitated response: "If rebels don't kill, then why does *this one* know how to launch the ships rockets?"

I rolled my eyes. Not at Susan, but at her question. So many people had been blinded by the A.R. "He and his fellow rebels were already trying to destroy Dewa Ruci when we had found their camp. They don't kill; they want to help."

She had replied hesitantly, saying, "Are you sure?"

I shrugged, not knowing if I even knew, truly. The cause I was fighting for, the rest of the world... it all seemed so black and white. What I wanted to do... if we succeeded... the average life span would be shrunken by four times. Was it really right? I replied by saying, "You can ask him yourself."

And she would ask Beau soon enough if everything worked out.

We continued walking down the empty halls. The white walls and silver, metallic floors reflecting the bright lights above. I shook my head. These hallways were what people didn't want to see. Something so perfect that it wasn't natural. It was built in our DNA to want the imperfect-perfect of nature. We loved it. We couldn't live

337

without it. Yet for some reason we had turned our world into these hallways.

I gripped my backpack tightly with sweaty palms. Susan was right beside me, and I felt safe with her. We were so close to the location, and I could feel my anxiety growing with each step forward. What if Beau wasn't where we had discussed? What if we were caught before we could have any effect? What if we killed more than we saved? However, I couldn't pay much attention to any of these questions, zooming throughout my head, because I had a job to do. As I and Beau had agreed: not for us, but for our children's children. For the future of mankind.

We soon arrived at the end of our journey through the large ship, the ceiling giving way to a gargantuan metal haul which towered above us. Susan craned her neck up, trying to comprehend the scale of the A.R.R. Herald. "It's a lot larger than it looks from the outside," Susan said. "Are we at the right place to meet *Beau*?" She said his name with deep dreading. She did not hate him; she just wasn't sure.

I peered around the dark room, looking for markers Beau had told me to look for. A metal suspender there, a massive bolt in that corner… it seemed to be the right place. I went up to the haul, putting my ear to it, and rapping on it as Beau had instructed me: *Rap-rap, pause, rap, pause, rap-rap.* I waited for a response, doubts suffocating my mind. Worries making my whole-body shudder. We needed to destroy that plant, if we didn't, we'd be stuck with the same horrid world I had come to hate. Sadly, so much had to go right for us to succeed, it didn't seem possible, yet it needed to be.

My ear still pressed against the cold metal, Susan waited timidly behind me, waiting for action. A sound came back from the other side of the wall. Two simple taps. Beau was on the other side, and he was ready. "Stand back," I told Susan.

339

She did so, stepping away to hide behind a large metal beam for protection. I removed the F.E.D., uncapping it and spraying it onto the wall in front of me. I did it at just the right height, so that water wouldn't come flooding in, but Beau could still climb through. The foam expanded rapidly, and I quickly ran back. It would continue expanding until it reached such a temperature that it combusted. This was our first violent act. I had been trying to not harm anyone by trying to help, but now I felt that that may no longer work. No matter how sorrowful, I might have to hurt people to save many. Only if it came to that, of course.

I hid next to Susan, crouching next to her, and putting one arm over my head, and the other around her. Just as I did, a loud explosion sent vibrations out through the entire ship, an ear shaking bang flowing along with the explosion. Shrapnel came flying in our direction, putting dents in the bit of metal which protected us. People would have definitely heard us, so we had to act quickly now. I pulled Susan up. Dust was sprinkled throughout her gorgeous hair, and mine was probably thick with it too. Smoke filled the room, and I coughed as it clogged my lungs, waving it away from me. Susan did the same, stepping in front of me to get her first look at Beau.

And as the dust began to clear, the sun shone through the darkness of the hole we had made in large rays. Beyond the smoking crater the F.E.D. had left, was the silhouette of a man, standing atop a small, one motor inflatable boat. He bounced up and down with every wave, floating closer and closer to us. He looked like a hero, and in a way he was. Beau, like me, Susan, and Darlin were all heroes in that way. Making a difference that would change the world. Anyone who ever even changed the world just one tiny bit was a hero. For isn't that what a hero is? Just a regular person who decides it's time for a change, that the world needs someone to protect it.

Beau's boat glided to the A.R.R. Harold and reached it just when the last bit of the smoke had dispersed. It touched the shattered haul with a soft bonk of the two metals colliding. When it had, Beau stepped over the thick walls of the ship, and over the carnage, speeding over to me, grabbing my arm and pulling me in for a large hug. He laughed loud and then shouted, "We did it Brian! We're going to be able to fix everything!" So much like Charlie, they would have gotten along well.

I wheezed from being squeezed so hard, just able to give Beau a pat on the back. I didn't want to get my hopes up, but I couldn't help thinking the same thing. We could do it! We could once again make the world a paradise. When he finally released me from his hold, I said, "We just started, however the fact that we even made it this far is a miracle. We owe it all to Susan." I gestured over to her as she backed up a few steps, eyeing Beau suspiciously.

She piped in. "I was told *you* killed my parents. Is that true?" she asked. I could tell how hesitant she was to even be close to the man in the blue uniform.

"Ma'am," Beau said, walking up to Susan, towering above her, the tension between the two building, "I've been with the cause I stand for since I was just a young boy. Not once did I, or any of my comrades kill unless we were being attacked. We have one goal, rid the world of its evil. Were your parents good people, ma'am?"

"The best," Susan replied, staring sternly into Beau's eyes.

Beau nodded, stepping back from Susan. "Are you aware of what's on Dewa Ruci?"

"Yes."

"Then you know why we must destroy it and anyone who stands in our way. I don't want to kill as much as you two do, but if the people we are going up against

343

had the chance, they would shoot you on the spot." Beau turned to me. "Either of you got guns?" He asked.

I held up Darlin's pistol.

He shook his head, handing Susan, and then me, two sub machine guns. "You'll need these," he said. As he passed one to Susan he said, "And thank you, for what you did. We needed you."

Susan didn't respond, she just looked down at her gun. I examined my own weapon, by doing so nearly bringing tears to my eyes. The one thing I didn't want to do was kill. And yet, I had too. For my son. I would do anything for him, and if I didn't do this, kids like him, all around the world, would never be able to see *life*. If I didn't do what I had to do, who would? If I had to destroy life, then so be it. If what I did meant that someday, somewhere, there wouldn't be death, just life and bountiful beauty, then it was all worth it. I would try my best not to kill, as I always did, but I had to destroy that last Cortezeon Plant. That last curse upon the Earth.

I gripped the cold metal trigger of my gun. Perspiration making my hands clammy. Tears still in my eyes, I looked at Beau for guidance. I looked at him for a long time, and he just looked back. He too seemed saddened by our current situation. Finally, he said, "We have to go, A repair team is already on their way to prepare the entrance we made. A notification was sent to one of their computers the second we blew the hatch. They'll be here soon, they'll have guns."

I nodded, looking down at my feet to find that a small bit of seawater was seeping into the ship through the hole. The window to the outside was high enough above sea level that the only water coming in was from the towering waves. Looking up, I caught Susan's gaze. She was deep in thought. What a time to walk the planet. A time when the greenery which had once made the world

345

amazing was gone. A time when instead of fighting to live longer, we fought to shorten our lives for the good of the world, and the species.

In all of the known universe, our one small species, the human race, is the only known one that purposely fights to preserve our planet. That was why we were only physically small.

"Let's go," I said. It was time to break free.

We started back down the long hallways side by side. Aiming our weapons in any of the corridors we passed. Susan was on my right, and Beau was on my left. Crouching low to the ground, we attempted to make as little noise as possible and listen for the sound of opposing feet. Enemies whom we tried to avoid, but we were prepared to come in contact with. The goal was to get to the bridge, and if Darlin had prepared it for us, make sure that Beau could destroy Dewa Ruci. He knew just how to hit that godforsaken island so that it would implode. So, me and Susan's jobs was to escort him. It was a plan me and Beau had planned precariously, a plan which had to work.

We edged around the corridors, trying to make our way to an elevator which would lead us to the fate of the world. We could only pray that Darlin had done his job as we held our guns firm. That weapon, I knew I would have to use. We had been moving for at least a half hour since we had let Beau on the ship, and it was most likely our presence was already known. That was why sooner or later the trigger would have to be pulled.

Humans are small and meaningless, but life, no matter its size, needs to be valued. It was the ideology that life can be spent that had turned the nation I had once worshipped into what it was today. I would live how Beau claimed the rebels lived: do not attack, just defend your beliefs. Of course, I was attacking the ship, but that was only because I was attempting to protect. Protect Tim, protect that last island of green, protect humanity from themselves. Maybe now people wouldn't understand, but in the future they would.

The three of us crowded into the elevator, Beau in the back, and me and Susan side by side, facing the empty corridors. The doors closed. We began to ascend, each one of us so nervous for what was to come. Susan just stood still like me, both of us too tense to move, but Beau, he hummed a tune. An ancient song. I looked over my shoulder at the curious man, Susan doing the same. "What's that song?" She asked as we climbed higher and higher.

Beau cracked a smile. "A song I don't think anyone remembers."

We were almost there. I grasped Susan's hand for comfort, though I think both of us needed to feel the warmth of another human. "How do you think we'll be seen… I mean, how will history remember us?" I asked her.

She squeezed my hand even tighter as the elevator began to slow. "Well," she said, staring into my eyes, "I think it doesn't matter. As long as what we believe we did was right. Maybe we'll be just be like that song. Maybe no one will even remember us." She then closed her eyes, allowing tears to roll down her cheek, and gave me a small kiss.

I closed my eyes as well, enjoying what might be my last joyful moment, a moment which my wife would be proud of.

The doors opened, and we peered into a large corridor, the ceiling supported by large pillars on either side. At the far end was the thick metal door of the bridge, sealed shut. And trying to break in were several people crowded around with guns, a metal battering ram, and all covered with thick armor. A soft ding told them we were behind them, and as they turned to see us, me and Susan gave one last look at each other, and then split off to the side to reveal Beau as well. "Bring it," he said.

I jumped behind a large support beam gracefully, while Susan fired a few shots into the confused men only to dive to the side opposite of me on the other side of the hallway. Beau on the other hand pulled out two large guns and began to unload on the enemies. It was time to make sure we didn't fail, even if we had to take lives.

Out of the fifteen people who had been attempting to get to Darlin in the control room (hopefully he had gotten there safely and wasn't dead) two had been hit by our shots. The remaining troop instantly began to get to their feet and protect themselves. They dropped the battering ram and started shouting at each other and shooting at the three of us. They barely acknowledge their dead; I reminded myself that was the reason for our revolt.

Beau was on the ground now, not dead, but lying on his stomach and still firing shots. However, the enemy fired back, their own bullets sparking off my protection and almost hitting Beau. I quickly peeked around the pillar, and got a few shots off, hitting a young man. I then beckoned to Beau. While distracted by my shots, he had time to run over to me and hide.

Susan had hit a few as well, and there were now ten men left. But now our attack had slowed, and we were pinned against our hiding places, me and Beau on one side of the hall, and Susan on the other. We needed Darlin and Charlie; we needed more than our small brigade of three people. Could we defeat an army, with such a small force of people? We needed those others, those who hid in the shadows and yet agreed with us. We were so outnumbered, so oppressed. Between shots, I could hear the other soldiers speaking about us: "One of those is the traitor, he already was captured once, what makes him think he can prevail?!"

"They only have three men; they won't get much farther!"

I couldn't let the odds get to me. We had to succeed, we would.

I shouted over the noise of bullets hitting metal that was only a few inches from me. "Beau, we need to do something soon! They probably already have backup coming!" I screamed.

He nodded, then we both looked towards Susan. She looked back, prepared to do whatever she could do. How strong she was. I held up my fingers so that both Susan and Beau could see. Three, two, one...

We rocketed out from where we hid at the same time. I crouched under Beau, slowly advancing with him and Susan, who was parallel with us. Light glistened in the shadows as we shot at our enemies only to get return fire. Beau had his two guns in each hand and held them above me, and along with me, we destroyed our competition. Bullets whizzed by me, but we continued charging into the unsuspecting soldiers.

Susan was having a harder time. As the only target on her own side of corridor, many shots went her way. I saw this and sprinted towards her. Sliding on the ground to grab a fallen man's shotgun. I continued sliding on the slick floor, and almost in slow motion, shot dozens of shells. I came to a stop right next to Susan, only to stand right back up and continue the fight. Soon, I was out of ammo, and noticing this, Susan ducked in front of me and proceeded by killing the last of the defenders.

The battle finished, smoke wafting int the air, I walked back to the center of the hallway with Susan panting. Beau was already crouched, moving the dead from the closed door. It hurt to slaughter people; the people whose blood covered the white marble floor. But we were one step closer.

After clearing away the caucuses, Beau stood back to be with us. We couldn't say anything about what we had just done, so all Susan said while staring at the metal hatch which concealed the control room was, "Should we go in?"

"There'll be more soldiers coming up soon. We better," I said, walking up to the mighty, metal door.

Beside me were the bodies of the fallen. I could hardly look at those men I had killed, but I would have to mourn them later. I banged on the cold metal saying, "Darlin, it's us."

We waited for a response. "You're sure your friend knows how to control these computers?" Asked Beau.

"It's his job. If you tell him how to destroy *Dewa Ruci*, he'll be able to do it," Susan said, her eyes wandering towards the corpses.

Soon, the squeaky voice of Darlin replied. A voice which only boosted my hopes that somehow, we would come through. "Brian! Hold on I'm coming!"

The door creaked open slowly, a timid Darlin peeked through the cracks. His eyes darting back and forth, speaking amazingly fast. "Brian, I tried so hard, but I just couldn't… I mean I truly tried my best… its just-"

"Darlin, Darlin," I said, trying to calm the man down, "what happened?"

He glanced around, wheezing heavily. He looked from me, to Susan, and then stopped for a second to look at Beau. He studied the man hard, but eventually said in a raspy voice, "Ok… come in."

We stepped into the control room, me right behind Darlin, and Beau at the back, weapon in hand. The scene inside the room was not unlike the hallway we had exited. Spread around the floor were even more dead men. Each one was stiff and bleeding. Darlin swept his arm around the room. "This whole place was teeming with soldiers," he sniffled, "I cleared them all out. It was working Brian. We were going to do it. But then people got word of *what* I was doing..."

"Oh my God," Beau muttered.

He was staring out the window, leaning against the high-tech computers to get a view of the destruction. Me and Susan walked over to him, awestruck by what we saw. Beneath us, rounds came our way, sending people flying into the sea when they hit. Above, planes bombed our carrier, yet neither time did we retaliate. "They sabotaged their own defenses!" Exclaimed Susan.

Among the battle, you could clearly see the wreckage of smoking anti-air-cannons, along with missile launchers. We had made ourselves defenseless in order to protect that one island. What had we become?

Darlin nodded to Susan's outcry. "They instantly destroyed all their gear. They could tell what we were trying to do. Now they'll die, but Dewa Ruci won't."

We were silent then for a while, listening to the sound of bombs being dropped on the carrier. Silent while the dead rotted. We had gotten so far, so close, now it was all over. Susan came up to me, tears in her eyes and gave me a hug. She may have just joined this fight, but I think she had always truly wanted to be a part of it. She wanted that better world. And so I cried with her, and so did Beau, and Darlin. None of us could grasp the fact that that green which we so loved would die. Our plan had failed, all because we had misjudged how insane the governments we fought, and their followers could be. We misjudged General Myer, President Kyle, Charlotte Hive, all of them. We had no idea how monstrous they truly were.

A larger bomb hit the deck. Without defense, the vessel was beginning to sink. We would die, and nothing could be done. I peered once more down to the water. There, bouncing up and down with each wave, was the small dingy that Beau had taken to get to the A.R.R. Harold. Was there a way?

I turned on my heels, forgetting my sadness, and trying to formulate a plan. "Beau, can't we get into Dewa Ruci, and destroy the *plant* that way?" I asked.

Beau wiped his tears from his eyes. "You could, but its highly armored, and we have no idea if someone is already there," said Beau.

"Hand me one of your guns," I said.

Beau gave it to me obediently. I began walking over the pools of blood, and towards the exit. "Brian, where are you going?" Susan asked.

I stopped, saying, "I'll take Beau's boat to Farm Outpost 1, we have no options left."

Darlin shook his head. "You don't know what you'll find there," he said.

Susan grabbed my hands, pulling them close to her chest. "Darlin is right, it's too dangerous."

I sighed. "If I don't do this who will. It is needed of me to do something. If I don't do this we'll die, so I must at least try. For my son, so that he'll have a chance to live. Not live like us but live for real. You must at least let me try."

"I don't know if I can…" she said. "Both of us have already lost too much."

I gave Susan a kiss and then let go. I spoke louder then so the room could hear, "I want all of you to get to the escape pods. Get home, if I don't make it, someone needs to watch Tim."

I walked on, trying not to think about what would happen if I didn't come back. "Brian," I turned back one last time to see Beau, the man who had helped me feel I could do something the man who had given me a chance at the last minute, "good luck," he said.

I nodded.

Running out the door, I followed the path we had used to get to the control room. Down the elevator and then winding through the hallways that made up the ship. Oh, how it hurt to leave, but I had to do something. A father will go to the ends of the earth to make a better like for his child.

Making it to the room we had blown a hole in; I was shocked to find it filled with water to the knee. Normally crews would already be down here filling it, but now I guess everyone knew their fate. I hopped through the hole and onto the small, one-motor raft, which was still floating right where Beau had left it. I started up the engine and sped across the angry ocean. The fumes from the motor suffocated me, the bouncing of the boat disoriented me, but I had to keep going forward. I could see Dewa Ruci on the horizon. A small rock jutting from the sea.

Underneath me, even through the dirty water that was filled with our pollution, I could see the outlines of monstrous creatures. Animals we had created yet would love to eat us alive. I sped over them, but they reminded me of the Cortezeon Plant. We had made this problem, and it was destroying us. Maybe we would survive, but morally we would never recover.

Humans need the sun, not just a cloud filled sky. We need trees, not a maze of buildings. We need life…not our own, but a thriving, amazing, beautiful planet. Without those things we are nothing. Too small to recognize.

Chapter 17

My boat hit the rocky island of Dewa Ruci just as the sun began to set. The metal scraped against the small island, and I stepped off onto an uneven surface, with cracks and crevices all over the black, slippery rock. There was almost nowhere to walk, and beside the raging ocean, there was the black door which had blended in with the rest of the island.

I had made it. After all the death, all the hardship, all the pain, all the time, all the distance, I had finally reached the ominous location. The place where I had been recruited to lead an expedition too, and the place where I would try to change things for the generations of the future. The world would be full of life again, and the people that fed off of the pain of planet would have nothing left to monopolize. However, floating amongst the rocks, besides my own boat, was an escape pod. The Tahoen flag painted on the side of it, along with the symbol they gave to high-ranking officials. It was empty, but I knew I wasn't alone on Farm Outpost 1, Charolette Hive was here. A person who just wanted to avenge her family, but in doing so was supporting another evil.

Having Beau's gun now, I grabbed onto the door and peered into the dark complex, making sure I was as silent as could be. If I ran into Charolette, I would make sure I got my *own* revenge. Nothing would stop me. I knew now the scale of which Dewa Ruci was on, Timmy's life depended on what I would do.

When I stepped into the room, white lights turned on and bathed the building. Allowing me to see everything, along with notifying Charolette, and anyone else that I had entered. The lights went all the way to the bottom of a massive staircase that went deep beneath the waves. I peered over the metal railing which was the only thing separating me from a painful fall.

I didn't sigh; I just started the climb. The stairs were rusted from years of being under the ocean, and water dripped from the ceiling, hitting the far-off ground with a small *plink*. It smelled of corroded metal. The tapestry of rooms which Beau had shown me were all far underground, and had been built so long ago, yet all the technology I saw looked so new, even if it was covered with rust. We had truly slowed our evolution.

Each step I got closer to the end, the more I wanted to run, to jump to the bottom and destroy that plant as soon as possible. But I stepped down slowly, each step carefully placed, trying not to make a single sound. And all I could think about was Susan, Darlin, and Beau. I had left them, and I needed them to be safe. What would I do if I made it and they didn't?

As I continue winding down beneath Dewa Ruci, the destroyed metal that made up the walls and stairs soon turned to a brilliant white, smooth design. Small branches of corridors began snaking out from the main shaft, leading to smaller, different holding shafts. White doors, the same shade as the rest of the facility, had windows which peered into the chambers. Some held vast stores of grain and the DNA of old animal life, others, super computers and blueprints. Each room's goal was to make sure humankind would thrive again. Whether that be with life, or knowledge. And the deeper I went, the more serious and complex the rooms became.

In one of these rooms, I stopped to peer into the window for a moment because something had caught my eye. On a prehistoric blackboard, the images, and math, showed what humanity were to do if the Earth became unfit to sustain us. It told us how to colonize other planets, how to make them our own, how to travel far in search of another world we could destroy. Like a virus, once one was destroyed, we would move onto the next. We used all of the Earth, and once it could give us no more, we would move on.

I started moving again. It was hard to pay attention to something so unbearably true. Something that showed what we really were. It pained me to even think about those things. To see that we all those dark thoughts in my mind which told me we were monsters might not be too far from the truth.

Glancing into every glass window carefully, I was nervous to see what I feared most. Charolette Hive and her guards, entering a room filled with Cortezeon Plants. But I peered in everyone slowly, only giving a slight peek to see if I had finally made it to the right chamber, and then moving on. I dreaded finding her, but I knew I needed to for the sake of us all.

The stairs stopped. Leaving me to look at a solid glass door, above it was a sign that read: *Cortezeon Plant*

Strain 2. After all the time I had spent trying to get where I was, I had finally done it. I had reached Dewa Ruci, and I *would* make a difference. A large one at that. Barely checking my surroundings, for I was so overcome with joy and pride, I ran in a dead sprint towards the door. When I came to it, I noticed that there was one door in a small enclave, with another door behind it, a type of air lock. Through the glass I could see the other side. Charolette wasn't there.

In fact, the room was deadly silent. It was solid glass, like the door, and even the floor and ceiling at this part. It was all completely see-through. Yet the only thing to see was the disgusting, polluted water of the outside sea. Rows and rows of leafy plants lined the walls of the room, almost exactly like the Cortezeon Plant except for an unnatural purple tint on the edge of their leaves. They stood still with no wind rippling through them, so unearthly.

Even their light came from bulbs, not even the real sun, for light couldn't break through the murky water.

I shoved hard on the door trying to open it. Not a budge. There was also no handle. Automated? I was so close now that I could almost touch the wretched plants, and that was all I wanted to do. Grab them and rip them into pieces.

A sound came abruptly, a screeching of glass moving, but it wasn't coming from in front of me. I turned around just in time to see the other door that made up the airlock closing, locking in place, and trapping me in a glass box. I banged once on the glass, trying to figure out what had happened, but my hand just ended up bruised. Then I heard a voice, the voice of someone I knew I would have to face eventually. "I'm sorry Brian," Charlotte said sullenly.

She stepped out from under the staircase I had exited and walked right up to the door which separated the two of us. I had rushed, and now I would pay for that mistake. Like the rest of the species, my flaw was overconfidence. Overconfidence that we could achieve anything. Charolette put one of her hands on the glass. Her eyes were watery, and she did in fact seem truly upset. When she spoke, she was muffled by the door, showing how truly thick it was. "We need this Brian, I'm truly sorry."

I took Beau's gun and smashed it against the glass, right where Charolette's face was. Still, there is not a scratch on the door though. "You killed Charlie, you killed people who had families, people who didn't want to get involved in any of this!" I screamed.

"The glass is bullet proof and controlled by a computer system on my side. This facility, though old, is highly technological. So, I suggest you listen," she said, her voice regaining more of its bite. I stood back, I would wait, listen, bide my time until I had the right moment. I would not forget what she had done. Nodding at my response, she continued, "You know, just as I do, that the battle which is raging above us will be the end of us all. The A.R.R. Harold is sinking, yet so is our own ship along with the Rohans vessel. I came here on an escape pod to retrieve Dewa Ruci's bounty so that we might use it to bargain our freedom. You do realize that I do this so *less* will die. You, on the other hand, came here for a different reason. You obviously know what's on Dewa Ruci now and hopefully see its importance. What do you say to that?"

"If you... came here... to convince me that what is in that room is good... is holy... then you've lost your mind," I grunted.

"We both hate the Andy Region, and we both know that if we take what's on the island their monopoly will fail. They've taken everything we love; we can defeat them!" She screamed back.

I shook my head. "The Andy Region isn't the only corrupt nation. That plant seems to destroy anything it encounters."

Throwing her hand in the air and taking a deep breath, she stared at me coldly. She was stuck. Like me she had begun to question everything around her. "Brian, you have a son. Why don't you want him to have a long and happy life?" She asked agitated.

I ignored her question completely, simply retaliating with my own. "Why haven't you killed me?"

Charlotte wiped her eyes. "Well, I... I..."

"You've seen it to," I said. "You can see nothings worth taking a human life. You see now that the plant was never meant to be found. That it is not a miracle, but a horrible omen. One which warns us to stop our wicked ways before it is too late."

She shook her head rapidly. "No! Your life is worth taking because getting that plant *will* bring peace. I can destroy the A.R. with it and finally avenge my family's death. What do you think would happen if we could no longer live three hundred years?"

"I feel the world would be better that way."

"You can't seriously think that."

"But I do."

Charolette trudged even closer to me, wagging her finger in my face. "People are being killed outside fighting over this island. If *we* take the plants, there will be nothing left to fight over. The death will stop."

I leaned against the glass, saying, "It won't though. If we release the Cortezeon Plant everyone *will* die. The A.R. isn't the only malicious nation. You really believe taking the plant will stop the fighting? That will only force nations to war even more… killing people like your family… like mine… like Susan's."

She brightened for a second, as if having an epiphany, ready to say something. But then her mouth hung open, she dropped her gun, and it clattered onto the ground she gasped for air. Choking, she fell against the door slowly and smeared blood on it. I tried to grab Charolette's falling hand, but my own bounced off the glass. She hit the floor, her head resting against the door, a pool of blood already forming beneath her. She was still alive, but her breaths came in short, rasping sessions.

Behind her, standing on the stairwell, was Susan. A pistol in her hand, and a plume of smoke shrouding her. She ran up to me, not even glancing at Charolette. "Brian!" She screamed. Susan pounded her fists on the glass. "How do I get you out?" she asked on the verge of tears.

I opened my mouth to respond but was silenced by Charolette. She had crawled away from me and now was leaning back on a corner. When looking at her, I saw something new, something that hadn't been there before... or at least something previously invisible. Had my words really changed her? She wheezed, "Control panel... top left..."

Susan glared at her but went over to the small pad on the wall beside me. "It needs a four-digit code."

Charolette coughed. "2086."

Susan typed it in quickly, her fingers speeding across the keys. With a sharp hiss, the door slid open, along with the one leading to the plants, and I ran into Susan's open arms. I gave her a large kiss and then we both looked down at Charolette. We had no time to love each other. People were being slaughtered, and the sooner we destroyed the plant, the thing which had ignited the war, the sooner the fighting could end. I asked, "What should we do with her?"

Lying there, looking up at the two of us with her large, sad eyes, Charolette said, "Leave me here to die… I…" She fell silent, not yet dead, but close to its icy grip. So close.

I turned to Susan, "Let's go in," I said.

We stepped into the other room, dragging Charolette behind us and setting her on the glass wall, not wanting her to die alone. She was a villain, but only because she had loved. Not a crime, just what every human longed for… the touch of another. Maybe one of the reasons we wanted to live forever. To feel the warmth of another, of many. By loving, she had always been human, but in her last moments she had thought like a human as well. All I wanted to do was bring back the joy that had filled the world, but was it worth it if I had to kill? Was it worth it if people, even how small they were, would never be able to see the world I wanted to create?

How many had to die before mankind would understand? Understand that death is not a worthy price for anything. I didn't even follow that. I had killed for my goal, and that was why I had to make sure I fulfilled what I sought to accomplish. So, how many had to die?

Me and Susan eyed the glass box which surrounded ourselves and the plants. It was like a fish tank, and it had trapped the world in its curse. We would attempt to destroy it though, and free the planet. Susan grabbed one of the Cortezeon Plant's leaves. "So, this is it. This is what we went to war for," she said.

I sighed, walking up to hold her hand and stare down at the horrible organism beneath me. "Like ourselves, it is extraordinarily small, but what it has done…"

"So, we must destroy it?" Susan asked. Like all of us, a life that goes on for hundreds of years was so enticing, but it wouldn't be living.

"This modified Cortezeon Plant may make us live even longer, we don't know. But yes, we have to destroy it," I said.

"Even if… Tim?"

I stood still, remembering my boy which I had set out on this journey for, thinking of his short life and how he was yet to take the Pill. He would die young, and if I survived, I would have to watch him leave me. I choked back a sob. "We still have to."

"So how do we do that?"

Charolette groaned in the corner and then sat up a bit. "…ventilation system…" she rasped.

Me and Susan both looked at each other skeptically. "How do you know all this?" Susan questioned.

377

Charolette smiled, her hand putting pressure on her own wound. "We… had planned our mission to this island… to the smallest detail," she took a gasping breath in between words. "If you destroy the ventilation system… with a timed bomb, water will rush in here, and then this whole structure will implode."

"You're sure?" I asked. We had come thousands of miles, done unspeakable things, I wasn't going to screw up now.

However, Charolette was staring off into space now, not able to hear my question. I looked around the room, attempting to find the ventilation system. I saw it. Tucked away in the corner of the room. "There it is," I said, pointing towards the small vent.

Susan gave me a puzzled look, asking, "We're really listening to her?"

I nodded, turning from the vent to look at Susan. Smart, gorgeous, sympathetic Susan. "At this point it doesn't matter what side people are on. If the human race wishes to survive, we must put aside our differences for the greater good," I spoke.

"But what if she's lying?" she asked.

I put my hand on Susan's warm cheek, I said, "Does it matter? Every second we waste someone is dying. It doesn't matter who or what someone supports, as long as they want the death to stop."

Susan smiled, a big, beautiful smile. "I still don't know how you see like that," she said.

"That's what makes the current world such a bad place. Everyone should see like this."

She kissed me.

We stepped up to the vent which was high on the roof. Everything. Everything we had worked for,

379

everything we had done, all of it converged onto this moment. We *would* change the world, and we *would* make sure the people of the future inherited a better world. "Do you have an explosive?" I asked.

Looking down at her belt, Susan fidgeted off a bundle of C4. "We can plant this and detonate it once we're out."

I left Susan to figure out how, and where to attach the explosive. While she was doing that, I wandered over to Charolette who was hardly even breathing. It hurt me to see another human being in such a state. Hearing my footsteps, she opened her eyes slightly and stared up at me. I didn't say anything, and I didn't think I could. The grief I felt, even for such a monster, was unbearable. "When you blow this place apart, leave me here," Charolette whispered.

I was taken back by the sudden heroism she showed. Leave another human to die… "Are you sure, don't you have people that…"

I was interrupted by her holding up her weak hand to silence me. "Let me die here. You were right Brian; I did see it. I saw what a monster I had been, I saw how what I did was not right, and I saw the right path. Life is not something that can be spent. I don't deserve to die up there. Die with people who see the right way." She stared to choke, and with her last breath, said, "Brian, you're doing the right thing… no matter what *they* say, and they will say things, remember that."

And then she was gone.

Another soul lost for all the wrong reasons. She would never be able to see the world we would create, as would so many others. So many dreams destroyed, so many families torn apart. And Charolette had said something that had got me thinking: "no matter what they say…" I had not made it through yet.

I would be persecuted, and people would curse my name. Yet I would stay strong. I had done so much, and I would not let any of it go to waste.

Tapping me on the shoulder, Susan awoke me from my trance-like thoughts. I was still looking at Charolette's body, and I realized that a lot of time had passed. "I planted the C4. We got to go," Susan said.

"Ok," I said, choked up.

We walked out of the horrible, ghastly chamber, and then hid behind the stairs. The door closed automatically behind us. Such an advanced system. If we were so advanced, why didn't we treat others like an advanced society would? We would follow Charolette's last wish, we would make sure that our mission was completed. "Blow the charge," I told Susan.

She clicked the remote, and a shudder went through the entire structure. From our side, we could see through the glass door and watched as black smoke filled the room. Consuming Charolette's body, and the Cortezeon Plants. Fire could be seen glowing against the background of fumes.

All I could think about was Charolette. Her sacrifice had made this possible. But time and time again I had said human life should never be bargained for your goal. Even a monstrous person like Charolette, someone who had murdered, didn't deserve this fate. When Susan killed her, though necessary, we had become just as bad as her.

But she had helped us, she had made it all worth it. Without her small influence, maybe we wouldn't have been standing where we were, watching as we re-wrote the world's story.

After a couple more seconds of the room filling up with smoke, a loud cracking sound started. It grew and grew and grew until finally, with a shattering of glass, the outside ocean came rushing inward. Swallowing everything in the cellar within moments. Charolette's grave was the sea, I would not forget what she had done.

And then, it was complete.

All the sacrifice we had put in had paid off. After all I had fought, after all I had worked for, after all the men I had killed, we had finally done it. That one explosion had washed away the blemish which had been on the Earth. The rest of the Cortezeon Plants would die, and with the death of them, the world would return to normal. Life would once again teem on the Earth, filling the waters and land abundantly. Tim would grow up in a world where people may be lesser, but they would treat each other with more respect. For I blame the plant, which's monopoly had once held the world, for people's loss of humanity.

However, anyone and everyone like me would be looked at with disgust for our opinions. Scolded for how we had changed the world. In the future maybe they would understand why we did what we did. None of it mattered as long as Timmy got a better life though.

I even thought of myself as the villain occasionally. Shortening people's lives. But what people were doing right now wasn't living.

So, me and Susan walked up the high winding stairs. All the way back to the peak of the small island. There was no more Dewa Ruci, we had only named it that because we needed something from it. Now that that thing was gone, mankind had no other need for Dewa Ruci. It was too small to matter anymore.

When we opened the door to the outside world, and the horrible, polluted air rushed in, I had to squint to block my eyes from the sun. The sun! Always hidden by clouds but not now! Now it was shining brightly through the clouds in rays that danced in the water. Finally, everything seemed to be looking good.

"Brian Watson, Susan Winter," we both looked down from the beautiful sky to see a battalion of Rohan soldiers surrounding us, there guns pointing at us both. All of them were clad in thick armor, armor only the best wore. Their sergeant was speaking to us, "You have been charged with a number of crimes against humanity." He frowned, saying, "I will never know why you did that."

I gripped Susan tight, pulling her close to me. Yes, many would hate us for what we had done.

Chapter 18

They were signing the treaty at exactly noon.

The A.R.R. Harold had long since sunk, along with the Tahoens' whole armada. Only the Rohans had made it out of the fierce battle, just barely, and we now stood on their only remaining carrier, the *Realization*. Chained to the deck and guarded by Rohan soldiers after being brought to their vessel, all as people looked at us with tears in their eyes and shook their heads. Rumors had spread, and some now knew what we had done. We had destroyed something people had given their lives for; we could not be forgiven for that.

President Kyle had even died. Killed in the fighting. Now General Myer was technically the highest-ranking officer, and for the time being, responsible for the Andy Region and its people. That meant he was also in charge of me and Susan, and before signing the treaty, he had come over to us unimaginably sad like the rest of the Realization. Even the Rohans, who had somewhat won the battle, seemed depressed.

General Myer had stood over me and Susan, our hands tied to the deck. He had little freedom on the foreign ship and seemed far off as he talked to us. He, like us all, had lost someone he had looked up to. "I hope you're happy," he had said.

Staring up at him, I replied, "I had no choice."

The general had just scoffed and sulked away. He would have to sign the treaty soon, and because of us, the treaty did not favor the A.R. But Myer knew we would be punished soon enough, so at the moment he made no attempt to harm us.

President Yang, leader of the Tahoens was the first to step up to the table where the treaty was. The large paper unfurled on the wooden desk as the waves rocked the boat.

We were outside, and the wind made the paper ripple with every gust.

Yang picked up the quill. Looking around at the crowd which had surrounded him, he seemed skittish. The treaty wasn't very good for him either. With the upper hand, only the Rohans would be keeping all their land. The Tahoens would lose a good portion of theirs, and the A.R., because of me and Susan and our *horrible* crimes, would be losing nearly half of their current empire. None of it mattered though. Each country relied on the Cortezeon Pill for most of their income. Soon, the last plant would die and the A.R. wouldn't be the only government to suffer. However, Yang signed the paper quickly, wanting to get away from the humiliating situation. He didn't have a choice. And so, one country gave into the Rohans. The soldiers gathered to watch seemed ready to cry. Occasionally one or another would glance at us and give us an ice-cold stare.

We were already heading back to San Francisco, and there we would be tried, along with Beau and Darlin, for *crimes against humanity*. Similar charges to that of what the Nazis had been charged with. *My* actions compared to that of the Nazis. I had to try my hardest not to break into tears. In fact, all I could do was look at Susan. However, seeing her despairing face just made things worse. If only Beau and Darlin were with us. They were being held in a prison below deck though. As for us, the world wanted us to watch as our country died. Maybe I would be stronger if they were with me, if all the people I had lost were next to me and Susan. Like the rest of the human race, we could endure more together.

Then General Myer stepped up to the pact. He seemed quivering with fear, the one man who would fight until his last breath was giving in. Picking up the pen, General Myer began to sign his name across his sheet. Half-way through though, he stopped. Looking up from the treaty, he stared at the two of us. His eyes were full of a fiery rage incomparable to anything else. "Why am I signing this?" The general asked. "Why am I being punished? Why are any of us? That one," he pointed at me, "he is the real monster! The rumors you have been hearing are true. He, along with his conspirators, has destroyed what may have been humanity's only chance of survival! The Cortezeon Plants are going extinct, and what may have been the only thing that would keep the species alive, he destroyed! We all were trying to help the world; he is the man you want!"

Two Rohan officers came up to Myer and pushed him into the table. "Just sign," one of them said. The general shook his head and then continued his signature.

Fighting the bonds on my hands, I cried out, "You don't understand! We-"

A soldier walked over and punched me in the jaw. "Shut up," she shouted.

I spit and blood came up. Everything I said was hated. Even when I was doing nothing, people looked at me like they wanted me dead. This was not what I had fought for.

A voice sounded off to my right. A loud, booming voice that made the shouting and screams of the vessel go quiet. "Silence!"

The man was King Harriet, a ghoulish old man, king of the Rohans, and the last to sign the document. He limped over to me, a wooden cane in hand. He had been injured in battle and truly despised us. The king towered over me, and glaring down towards the two of us, he said, "Not one of you is to lay a finger on these *disgusting* people. The general spoke truthfully, but they will be tried once we get back to North America. Just wait. Their time will come."

King Harriet stumbled away to the table, and in one swipe of his hand, signed the treaty. I could see from the corner of my eye General Myer. He was sitting on the concrete deck alone. Everything he had worked at was gone. All the money he wanted, the fame. Can't you picture the title which he had sought? *Hero Saves the World!* He now would only get recognized for his loss. The general would have had it all. Now he had nothing. Like the rest of us he would just have to adapt to a world where you had to think of others. That would be how we survived.

I could hear everyone around us muttering, shooting evil looks at us. They wanted to kill us, hang us, make sure that people like us disappeared from the Earth. The worst thing was that I had dragged Susan into my problems along with Beau and Darlin. Each one of them would be persecuted for what they had believed in. Because of me they would die.

. . .

The Realization sped across the sea. Through storms, towering waves, pitch black nights, the Rohan boat always kept moving. And no matter how harsh the conditions, me and Susan were left chained to the concrete deck. All we had was each other, and maybe that was enough.

Rain would come down on us in raging torrents, but we were together. While everyone else was safe inside of the bouncing ship, we were stuck on deck while waves crashed onto us. And all we could do was attempt to hold onto each other and try not to die. We couldn't speak because of the ear blasting wind, but we didn't want to. For all we could think about was our fate. What would happen once we were put on trial?

I think we both knew what the outcome of the trial would be. They said we would be tried with crimes against humanity! Just hearing that, people would think we had done something truly horrible, and maybe we had. What made it even more terrible was the fact that Susan would now go down in history as a monster.

However, when I looked at Susan. Her hair wet, water dripping down her chin, I realized something. She was not weak. Even with the terrifying waves coming down on us, she held fast. She was shivering, but she clenched her teeth so the enemy would not see her pain. She was so strong. I hadn't made her come with me to destroy the plant; she had come because she knew what was right. How strong she was.

And that was why I felt such a strong bond between us.

I wanted tremendously to just wrap my arms around her and hold her until the end of the storm, but alas, chains bound us. Made it so we had no room to move, no room to grow as people. Yet, they were the only reason we weren't thrown overboard. That was why the chains were just like what the Cortezeon Plant had been. Something binding us down. Something that had made sure we couldn't love or appreciate what the world had to offer. Yes, maybe without the plant we would have to struggle in a raging sea, but what was life if you were trapped?

Somehow, through the harsh conditions and malice filled men, we made it. I am unsure how, but we did. One day, upon waking up from a restless sleep, my clothes soaked in filth, I saw it. The coast. An unnatural, grey, concrete coast which blended with the water and the sky to make one hideous block of death. Yet in that moment, I was filled with such incredible joy to be home that I cried. Never had I ever been so happy to see the concrete jungle I called home in my life. When looking at the jagged, man-made California coast it was as if I could see Tim staring back at me. I nudged Susan, awakening her to see the hideous and gorgeous site. We both knew it was our doom, but it still felt like home. And though we were so far offshore, I could have sworn the speck of green was just barley visible amongst the smog.

Soldiers began to venture on deck on the relatively clear morning, not in good moods, but happy just as we were to see land. They still followed us with deathly eyes, occasionally cursing us, but mostly they just kept to themselves and watched the land grow larger as we sailed to port. Something was strange about the scene, however. It was as if with every person who came on deck, the ship became quieter. As if some unspoken rule was in place to stay silent. Like a storm was brewing and no one wanted to make a sound to trigger the thundering clap of lightning and terror.

Soon, King Harriet came up as well, refraining from looking at us and just watching the coast. He seemed deep in thought, and just like the others, did not make a sound. But the ship kept moving, sailing under the rusting Golden-Gate Bridge and past the apartment complexes of Alcatraz, yet still the silence hung. Not even the gulls, which had been following the ship, spoke. The sea creatures that had glided alongside the vessel were now gone. The only noise: the engines which pushed us closer. Death seemed to hang in the air.

Finally, the Realization pulled into dock, shutting off its mighty engines and extinguishing the last sound. Guards came up to un-cuff me and Susan; Darlin and Beau were nowhere to be seen. I gave Susan a quick glance, trying to get a look at her gorgeous face and see what she thought the chaotic, deafening quiet was. But her face was too covered in grime. I assumed mine was as well. No words were spoken, and when the guards pulled us towards the vessel's edge (without any bindings for we seemed too weak for escape), I was able to see what was happening.

Beneath us, on the dock, along the streets, on the shore, in air taxis, upon the skyscrapers, in schools and homes, in places of business and in churches were people. So many people. They filled up every corner of the city and then some. They divided it in half. One side looking at the other, looking at the two of us. All too afraid to move. Eyeing each other from across the room and it was hard to tell who was on what side. Everyone was just silent. Not a sound but the crashing of plastic on the concrete beach. One looking at the other, neither wanting to make the first move. Some held signs thanking us, others, signs wanting us to hang. Of course, what caught my attention the most was those thanking us. What we had done had drawn the timid out of hiding. Yet still, I could barely tell the difference between the people. Each one had a bloodthirsty lust in their eyes. They were so incredibly different, yet the same. So divided in their beliefs, yet in union by their hatred.

What triggered the first act of violence I cannot say. A cough from someone disapproving of me? A sneeze from a supporter? Maybe even one stepping on the others foot? Whatever it was, the silence which had previously encompassed the population was torn down by what I can only describe as a storm. A horrible, violent, evil storm.

In a fraction of a second a riot broke out, and the peace was gone. First came the screams, then the stones, and finally the attack. Men and woman of both sides clambered up the boat, fighting and consuming in their tsunami of flesh whoever stood in their way. Before I knew it the ship was overrun, and beneath me, even more were dying, and in the city, fires were ablaze. This was no good versus evil conflict; this was just death. Death for something that had already happened. Death because of me.

Yet there was no time to give thought to morals and to ponder what I had done, for already the soldiers were being overrun. Bullets were shot into the crowd but that did little, the crack of guns was barley audible over the now roaring city. Our guards were quickly taken out, and in a second, we were free. Freed by friendly or foe, it did not matter which, we were just free. Free as the rioters overtook the Realization and it was flooded not just by people, but by the ocean. I looked out into the destruction which had suddenly engulfed the city, grabbed Susan's hand and ran through the crowd.

At the time I did not think of Beau or Darlin (I pray they made it out alive though they probably did not), nor did I think about where I would go (though I think I knew), all I could think about was Tim. Caught in a raging inferno which the city had become Caught in a battle of my own creation. So, I ran. Ran with Susan in hand as fast as our weak bodies could take us. Bolted through the chaos and the death all around me, through the truly terrifying mass of humans. Sprinted to my son who was trapped in a burning skyscraper. Dodged those who hated me and hunted me and tried to kill me, and upon finding my boy, wrapped my hands around him and swore never to let go. We escaped to the hills, not looking back at the burning city, at the burning kingdom, at the death. I cut through the chainmail fence that led to my paradise, my freedom, and pulled Susan through the last straggling claw the A.R. had around me.

I escaped.

I cried.

I loved.

I became, truly, a free man.

After all the many years I had lived, I had finally become human.

A Long While Later

Chapter 19

"Honey, come down for breakfast!" Susan shouted from the floor beneath me.

I rolled over onto my side. My old back hurting from our lumpy mattress. Something I would not have complained about when the whole world had been messed up. Now however, the little things seemed more important than ever.

Sighing, I sat up and looked at our darkened room. Susan had gotten up well before me but had left the blinds closed to let me sleep in, hiding the beautiful outside world from my view. I could smell breakfast cooking in the kitchen below. Susan made the best eggs, and that was only one of the reasons I was the luckiest man alive.

Grabbing my cane which was lying beside me on a small wooden dresser, I hobbled over to the bathroom to freshen up as I did every day. I parted my gray hair to one side in the mirror and then limped downstairs, attempting not to put pressure on my bad leg. When I came out from the stairwell and into the brightly lit room, Susan greeted me with a kiss. "Good morning, love," she said.

I returned the gesture and spoke, "Breakfast smells amazing."

"Thank you, I made it with you in mind."

I then just stared into her eyes. Her pretty green eyes, partially covered by wrinkles, and staring right back at me. Thirty years ago, today. That hurt to think of. That time was nothing compared to my long life, yet for the current generations a good chunk of theirs. What could I do to pay my homage if his death had been my fault?

"Brian, is everything all right?" Susan asked, stroking my chin softly with her puny hand, shrunk from the many years she had lived.

How old we were, it felt like only yesterday the Fall had begun, when we had been criminals. Now, those same crimes were looked at in a very different view. Now, all I could do was look at Susan's gorgeous face and let tears roll down my cheek. I still pictured the old woman, as old as me, as the "young" girl I had started another family with. We had had many children in a world where people lived short, yet full lives. Those same children were long dead however, and all that was left was their children, our grandchildren. Not one of them had been able to take the Cortezeon Plant and had died like normal people. For a parent to watch their own children die...We were cursed to live out our days watching those we love leave this world for what felt like eternity. That's what hurt the most.

Noticing my pain, Susan said, "This is what Timmy would have wanted. Now come and eat, they'll be here to pick you up soon."

I reluctantly walked into our amazing kitchen located at the back of the cozy log cabin in order to have my plate loaded with food. It was just like the rest of our amazing house, and the amazing world we had helped create. But sometimes, it felt that none of it mattered, especially when I remembered the price it had cost to build such a wonderful world for future generations. I stepped out into our living room and looked out the large glass window and onto the green forests beneath me, a forest that had grown from decay and destruction and death. The collapsed skyscrapers and most of the city, overrun with life. What remained of the wreckage was now covered in an infinite green which seemed to have no end. Teenagers would occasionally play in the abandoned, overgrown buildings, never knowing truly how ominous they were for those from that time. Was it worth the cost?

It had not just been the riots on that fateful return home that had caused the fullness of the Fall. No, it was also due to the collapse of the economy, which had led to other nations suffering similar fates. The A.R. had collapsed the fastest of course, what with the riots and all. And if it hadn't been for the secluded cabin I was in, my family might not have survived the fallout of my own actions. It had happened all so quickly… structures and empires falling. But the Earth had reclaimed them. Animals and plants now flourished, and throughout the newly rebuilt society, people had changed. Most of the time for the better. But at what cost?

Friends, family, loved ones… my choices had cost me those. Those things I would never get back. Beau, Darlin, Charlie… all dead. All dead because they had chosen to help me, because they had believed in me. Kate. I had promised her I would make a better world for our boy, for Tim… But Timmy had not had a choice. No one had asked him if he only wanted to live for several decades. If he wanted to die while his own father endured. I had made the decision for him…was it worth it?

Today, I would honor my son though. Go to his gravesite, and talk to him and Kate, and all those I had lost for what was probably the last time.

Tim had loved me even after what I had done. What an amazing kid.

To have lived through such a chaotic epoch, to have been hated by so many, it was ironic that it would be old age which would finally take me. And would I be missed? Well, after years of being persecuted, it felt as if people had begun to accept what we had done almost a hundred years ago. People had died, and people had been born. The new life seemed to be a lot different than the old. The next generation thought of their fellow man much differently than people of my time did. The children of the new world cherished every second they had to be alive, and in doing so, tried to make the world a place they wanted to live in. Everyone respected each other and made sure that the Earth was ready for the next generation.

Alas, how I wished the people of my time could have been thinking that way. If we had, maybe Tim would have had a better life. Maybe we could have kept the Cortezeon Plant.

I took a bite of my breakfast, letting the salty flavor soak into my tongue before swallowing. Even the food had changed since those horrible times. It felt cleaner, fresher, less corrupted. The world outside was miraculous, I only wished more people were here to see it.

Interrupting my thoughts, I heard a knock on the door and then Susan shouting, "Brian, your escorts are here!"

I set my plate down on the floor beside me (an unhealthy habit I had developed) and walked over to Susan to give her a goodbye kiss. Doing this, I then opened the door to look out upon two young nursing home caretakers. They were funded by the new state, the name of which constantly slipped from my old, tired mind. "Hello Mr. Watson, will the Mrs. be joining us today?" One of the caretakers asked me. Her name was Bella, a tall, young woman who, like the other officer, had taken me out on occasions similar to this. A very nice girl.

"No," I replied, "she insisted that I got to spend some alone time with my son."

The man beside Bella nodded. I remembered him as Randy, a small man with a freckled face and brown hair. He asked, "You ready to go then?"

I think I said yes, but at that point, when we were walking across my green lawn to the shuttle, all I could think about was Bella and Randy. They knew me, and I knew them. They knew very well what I had done, and yet still treated me like another human being. The rest of the world even seemed grateful for what I had done.

All I could think of today was how much everything had changed. It was probably just because it was the same day Timmy had died, and all I could think about was that he was missing. But had I not once said with Beau: *not for us, but for our children's children.* It was just that that was hard to accept sometimes.

Before I knew it, I was already in the large, all white land vehicle (air taxis had gone out of style), pulling out of my driveway. Leaving behind a small cabin and the pine forest it resided in; we soon entered the suburbs around my home. Even the places where people once lived had changed. Apartments becoming regular homes with green yards! It was all so different, and all of it was because of me and what I had done. People walked around the neighborhood walking pets and children, each one of them seemed so happy. So much change in such a short amount of time.

We drove on with not much conversation, driving through the big city (not so big now), and making our way closer to the coast of San Francisco. Looking out my window, it seemed as if the city had advanced more in just a few years than it had in my entire life. We left the metropolis though and got on a small coastal road. So many trees, so much life, so much happiness. Even if mankind wasn't as plentiful, you had to admit, it was a gorgeous world. Dense fog covered the land, obstructing our view just as it had that day I went on a conquest for Dewa Ruci.

How little I knew that day. Maybe that was the one blessing immortality gave you; you got to live longer and gain more experience. Yet people of my day were ignorant, especially in how they treated people. We could advance all we wanted, but there would still be those who were cruel.

Like General Myer, or the late President Kyle. Sometimes I even did things that just weren't right.

Soon, we were parked in a dirt lot outside of the cemetery. The engine of the rusty shuttle rumbling, both Bella and Randy looked back at me. "We can wait in the car while you go see you boy, if you like," Bella said.

"Ok," I replied.

I opened the door and stepped out, leaning on my cane to support me. Taking a deep, rasping breath with my ancient lungs, I smelled the sea air among the smell of pine. Salty. It almost made me laugh. After all this time the Earth had returned to its natural, perfect glory. It was time to pay my respects to Tim.

Climbing up the dirt trail to the graveyard, I couldn't help but appreciate such a dreadful place's beauty. Pure, morning dew covered the nearby pines and grass, and putting my cane on the final step right before the metal threshold, I looked over to see the sun sending beautiful beams of light shining like halos against the tombstones. I stopped to catch my breath, once again feeling my age, and then continued walking, trying to find my son. He was tucked away in the corner, right next to Kate and Charlie.

When I reached them, I gave my legs a rest by sitting on a bench situated in front of their graves. Kate's and Charlie's stones didn't have much written on them, but on Timmy's it was written: *Beloved son. Taken younger than most but loved more than anyone else.*

I looked between each of the gravestones. How I cared about each of the people in front of me. And how depressing it was that none of them were able to see such a wonderful place. A blue bird flew past me singing a lovely song. Yes, what a wonderful world. But then I looked back inland and saw the remnants of the old buildings. We had almost destroyed it all. Our arrogance, and our pride, and our belief that we could have anything and everything.

Even immortality on Earth. All of that had almost destroyed it all.

Letting the sun warm my old body, I stared down at my family. Timmy, I would always love him. Kate, I would always love her. And Charlie, he was one of the few people who I believe would have supported my cause just like Susan had. Just like Beau and Darlin, and all of those killed in the riots had. Each one of them I wished to be alive, but it would never be. We could postpone death all we wanted, but at the end of the day, we would die no matter what we did.

Then, knowing fully that my caretakers could hear me from their vehicle, I began to talk to myself while looking down at my dead beloved. I said, "Human beings can believe that they are all powerful, that they are the center of the universe... but death. Death will always be there to remind us just how small and insignificant we are."

416

THE END

Acknowledgements

I would like to thank you, reader, for finishing *A Familiar Future*. It has been an emotional journey to get here, and I can't thank you enough. There were tears of joy and sadness throughout my writing journey, and my only motivation was to know that someday, someone might pick up my work and read. I was born in 2011, so for someone to actually be exploring my work (and hopefully enjoying it) means a lot to me. A big shout out to my editor, Eric Smith, and everyone else who has helped my dream become a reality. I plan on writing much more in the future. Thank you once again.

Sincerely, Parker J. Hilton